ROUNDABOUT

A CREEKWOOD NOVELLA

A. MARIE

Editing: Sarah Plocher, All Encompassing Books
Proofreading: Judy Zweifel, Judy's Proofreading
Cover Design: Murphy Rae
Cover Photography: Cadwallader Photography, LLC/Utterly Unashamed, LLC
Cover Model: Jordan Ashlee
Formatting: Champagne Book Design

PLAYLIST

You can find the full playlist link as well as bonus material and inspiration boards on my website amarieauthor.com.

Happy Place—SAINT PHNX, Jasmine Thompson

Carefully—Demi Lovato

All Comes Back To You—R3HAB

Alarm—The Score

What If—YVR

My People (We Ready)—Hidden Citizens, Bryce Fox

Healing—FLETCHER

Thank You—Diana Gordon

This Is the Beginning—Ely Eira

Collide—Rachel Platten

Truly Madly Deeply—Chlara

ABOUT THIS BOOK

Roundabout is a 31k-word novella in the Creekwood series and centers around *Detour's* couple, Coty and Angela. It takes place six years after the epilogue in *Blind Spot* and features the rest of the crew. All books in the series—*Detour, Changing Lanes,* and *Blind Spot*—can be read as standalones, but being that they're interconnected, it's recommended you read the trilogy before starting *Roundabout* to avoid spoilers.

Roundabout: not using a short direct route but a longer, more complicated one; circular intersection consisting of multiple route options

CHAPTER 1

Coty

HANDS ON MY HIPS, I STAND BACK TO GAZE DOWN the middle of our two rows of apple trees, inhaling the rich combination of earth and growth and hard work. After years of babying these things, they finally produced fruit this year. It's a little late in the season now, so most of the apples were already picked and used, but I brought Jace out to see if we could find any stragglers to take over to Marc's petting zoo. With no breeze today, the buzz of bees fills the calm air, and I study one flitting close to my three-year-old since we don't know if he's allergic to stings or not yet. Jace flinches away from the bee, his shoulders up to his ears as his little body starts to shake. With a gentle tone, I talk him through the fear, reminding him this kind of bee isn't really interested in us, and as long as we leave it alone, it'll leave us alone. Once the bee moves on, Jace relaxes and focuses on trying to twist an apple off a branch exactly how I've been showing him for the last few weeks. Almost instantly, he loses patience and jerks on the fruit with all his might, falling right on his butt with a whiny groan...until he looks down at his full hands. Proud of himself, he smiles up at me and holds out the apple with only a few brushes of vibrant red across its mostly golden-yellow skin.

That puts us at two. Two apples for the goats. If I cut them small enough, they should last a good ten to twenty seconds, and that's if Marc's cow, Marcus, doesn't wander over, getting his fill, too.

"Way to go, buddy," I tell my son with my own smile, not only for persevering with the apple but also for keeping his cool with the bee. I know how scared he gets.

We got assigned to Jace a week after he was born. Our first time seeing him was in the NICU while the poor guy was coming down off crack cocaine and God knows what else. The month that followed was one of the longest of our lives as we watched him go through withdrawals. He's been doing great ever since but one of the long-term effects is bouts of temporary phobias. Angela and I adopted him outright but it took over a year to finalize because he was placed with us as what's called a legal risk placement, which means his biological parents could've taken him back with good behavior. It happens all the time. It just happened to us last month with a pair of sisters we had living with us for almost a year.

"Alright, let's go to Uncle's and see the goats."

The apple falls from Jace's hands, rolling a few feet away as he pushes himself to standing, chanting the word, "goats," under his breath. As soon as he's up, he's off, one arm pumping faster than the other as he charges full speed ahead.

In the opposite direction.

Without his apple.

Chuckling, I bend down to scoop up the forgotten apple, then jog alongside my kid to scoop him up, too.

"Not so fast," I say against his cheek, his greasy curls tickling my eyelashes enough for me to blink. He needs a bath. A real one. Soon. Drains are Jace's current phobia. Well, his biggest one. Sponge baths have been keeping his body clean but not his hair—unfortunately.

"Fast," he repeats. "Daddy fast."

"That's right." I get him situated in the crook of my elbow so I can look him in the eye. "Daddy's fast."

"Mommy fast?"

"A little," I say with a smirk, knowing if this gets back to her how offended she'll be.

"Oh." Jace's face falls like I just delivered extremely disappointing news. "A wittle fast?"

"Yup, only a little fast. She used to be faster." Decade-old memories surface, back when Angela used to run at the first hint of trouble, and I shake my head to clear it. Thankfully, it's been a long time since she's pulled anything like that.

"Oh?" He perks up a bit, playing with the collar of my shirt. "Why?"

"Because she doesn't need to be anymore."

"Why?"

I laugh at the reminder we're not quite out of the "why" phase all toddlers go through, then sober thinking of a way to explain it. This conversation took a deeper dive than I was expecting.

"Because Mommy doesn't have anywhere else she needs to go. She has everything she could ever want right here." I snuggle him closer, my forehead against his. Angela does love our life. She loves us. She loves me.

Not enough to marry me, even after being together every day for the past ten years.

She hasn't tried to leave me since our Creekwood days at least, so that has to count.

It does. It counts. She loves me.

I lower my voice to add, "And because Daddy's faster."

Jace's small, dirty hands pat my cheeks. "Daddy fast."

"Daddy's *faster*," I echo since the more times I say it, the greater my chances are of him repeating it back to his mother.

God, I hope she lets me have it. I fucking love when Angela's fired up, thinking she needs to prove herself. I already know what she's capable of, but I could go for a reminder. Or two. She may not be my wife—yet—but she's the living embodiment of every fantasy I've ever had.

◆ ◆ ◆

Before I can even kill the engine, Beck's brand-new Suburban High Country is already pulling in right behind me and parking next to my Camaro ZL1. He probably spotted me heading this way and invited himself right over. His twins, Terra and Harley, practically lunge out of the silver SUV, and jet straight for my driver's door, yelling, "Uncle Coty! Uncle Coty!" from the other side of the window. They have way too much energy, just like their dad.

Marc approaches us carrying his daughter, Blaze, and I give him a *can you believe this?* expression through the windshield. Smirking, he just shakes his head at me.

We see each other's families almost every single day but the kids always act like it's been months, if not longer. The younger ones anyway. The older ones…they're over us already. As long as we chauffeur their asses around, they're okay being in our company, otherwise not so much. For Hunter being an official high schooler now, he's not too bad, I guess, but Rebel… She's too busy running with her group of friends to hang with us anymore.

It's sad, how fast our street cred fades. We used to run shit, now we just run our kids around to their own shit.

At least we still have nice rides.

After unbuckling Jace from his car seat in the back, I help him climb over the center console, on to my lap, then slowly, we get out, careful not to clip one of Beck's kids with the door. Terra immediately takes Jace from my hands, walking him over to Marc and Blaze. Harley sticks around awkwardly like he's too cool all of a sudden, so I ruffle his light brown hair, hugging his head into my side.

Beck's the last to join us, and as usual, he's wearing one of his biker shirts, this one reading *I hate being sexy, but I'm a biker, so I can't help it* and I wonder what his wife said when he put it on this morning. Dude is asking for unwanted attention with that statement.

"What's up?" Beck asks with only his hands.

Since Blaze is here, everybody switches to signing. We all made the collective decision to learn sign language a little over five and a half years ago when Marc's little girl was born deaf.

I release Harley's head to answer, "Just here for the goats."

"Goats," Jace says by making a fist while crooking two fingers and tapping his chin then his forehead. Goats might've been his first word to ever sign. These goats are like magic. I knew calming goats were a thing for racehorses, but I never would've guessed they worked on kids, too. I'd have some over on my property if I thought they'd leave my produce alone. Since they seem to eat anything and everything, I leave the animals to Marc. I've got the crops, including the pumpkin patch we gave all the kids a hayride around earlier this month before letting them pick and decorate pumpkins; Marc's got the petting zoo and racetrack we all visit whenever we feel like it; and Beck's got the pool everybody swims in all summer long.

Terra and Harley each take one of Jace's hands, leading him over to the goat pen.

"Okay, not to be dramatic—"

My eyes are already rolling. Beck's main mission in life is to be as dramatic as possible.

"—but who the…" Beck drops his hands and mouths the word "fuck" before continuing signing, "…stinks? It better not be one of my kids."

How can he even tell it's coming from one of the humans? We're right next to a goat pen.

Blaze removes the arm around her dad's neck to ask "What?" with both hands.

I hit the back of Beck's head, then tell him, "Good job." By not signing it, Beck thought Blaze wouldn't catch the bad word he was using, but he forgets our niece can lip-read, too, and now he's got her curious about the word her uncle just mouthed.

He does it to himself, I swear.

Marc says, "Silly," using a fist with his thumb and pinky sticking out and wiggling it in front of his face.

Beck repeats the motion to Blaze, agreeing, "Funcle's silly." Funcle doesn't translate in ASL exactly, so he just uses the sign for uncle of his pointer and middle fingers up by his temple, but we all know what he means. There's not a day that goes by where he doesn't go out of his way to remind everyone just how fun of an uncle he is.

He says, "Don't use that word," with a blanching expression, then, "That's my word." He grabs her from Marc's hold and tickles her while giving her face a dozen kisses.

Blaze's laughs don't really make a lot of sound, but damn, are they fun to watch.

Even the kids know to sign all their words around their

cousin, but Beck…will always be Beck and try to bend the rules so he can act a fucking fool.

"Aunt says it," she says once Beck's done. Blaze's dark brown, almost black, hair is the only feature she seems to have inherited from Marc. Her face, including her blue-green eyes, are almost an exact carbon copy of her mom's. Through those eyes, she watches the world, understanding it in ways others can't even grasp.

Beck's eyebrows lift as he passes her over to me so he can ask, "Aunt Paige?"

Blaze nods.

"Aunt Paige is gonna get a spanking," Beck says.

Marc and I both groan. *Too far.*

Blaze gives me a questioning look, but I just shake my head, reminding her that Funcle Beck is silly with the same sign my friends just used.

I press a single kiss to my niece's forehead before putting her on the ground, giving her the bag of apple chunks from my pocket, and telling her to share them with the others.

"No luck getting Jace to take a bath?" Marc asks as we turn to watch our kids at the pen, this time on the outside of it. I don't see Hunter anywhere otherwise they'd all be *inside* the pen, "helping" him take care of the goats.

Beck was right, my kid stinks, but he didn't have to be a dick about it.

"No. No luck," I say, still signing, too, even though none of the kids are paying attention to us. It's easier that way, in case Blaze turns around.

"Bring Jace over to my house and stick him in my pool," Beck suggests. "I just gotta crank the heater for a day or two first."

"He's scared of a tub drain. How do you think he'll handle your pool's skimmers?" I ask Beck, because I know there's at least three on that beast.

"We can take him through the car wash in Angie's old Jeep like we did that one time."

"Does it even run still?" Marc frowns as he lifts a bucket full of pellets and deposits it next to the kids since the apples are gone already. I knew they'd go quick.

Once we started fostering kids, Angela finally upgraded to a new Jeep Grand Cherokee, this one with actual doors and windows, putting her 1986 CJ-7 out of commission for good. It's still at our house. I just haven't started it up in a long time. I've had my hands full with running my own design company as well as keeping up with the many kids we've had in and out of our house. Oh, and tending to the acres of crops I planted before our life started taking one busy turn after another.

"I can get it running long enough," Beck says before rubbing his hands together.

"We're not using the car wash." Angela didn't exactly appreciate the first time we did it, and that was just the three of us, not her son.

"If it wasn't so cold, we could just hose him down out here like we used to do to Hunter," Marc offers.

Some of our falls are warm, but this year isn't one of them. For it being only October, it's already cold as shit out.

"Where is your boy, by the way?" I ask him. Hunter basically lives with his goats, so I'm surprised he's not out here now.

"Fall Fest, setting up for this weekend. Want me to call Rebel? See if she's around?"

"No. Wouldn't want to impose."

We all share a laugh. Even when Rebel's not on her dad's racetrack, beating anyone dumb enough to challenge her, she's still going full speed, never easing up on the gas for even a second. We used to think our trio was crazy...'til Rebel's trio came along.

"Shit, I'll impose," Beck mumbles under his breath, his phone pulled out with his thumb already flying across the screen. "I'll text that little shit right now and tell her to get home to help feed these four-legged zombies."

Along with one of the biggest fucking hearts, dude's also got the biggest fucking head.

Terra turns around to tell her father, "That's fifty cents in the swear jar, Dad."

Sticking his phone between his ribcage and his bicep, he says, "What? I just put twenty bucks in that thing yesterday."

"You used it up already," Harley says.

To us, Beck mouths, "Fuck," all over again, this time making us chuckle. The way he cusses, that jar's gonna pay for both twins to go to college.

Back to using sign language, he asks, "Why is one looking at me while licking his lips?"

"Which one? Vincent van Goat?"

Marc chips in, mocking, "Or is it Chewy?"

"Neither, man. It's Stewart. Dude's a mess. Look at him." Beck points at Stewart, the white goat with his head sticking out of the fence, eyeballing us with those creepy-ass rectangular pupils.

"He's not a mess. That's literally what all the goats do. They stand there and eat and stare at anyone who comes out here."

Marc nods, adding, "And faint," since the goats he bought his stepson are the fainting kind.

None of us need to point it out but I know we're all thinking it: *and shit*. Goats shit everywhere.

After retrieving his phone, Beck frowns at it before tucking it back in his pocket.

Our niece probably responded, telling her uncle "no," which isn't exactly in Beck's vocabulary.

It's not really in any of ours.

"Too bad none of us have an indoor pool," our blond friend says before bending down to help flatten the hand Jace is holding out so the goats won't get a finger in addition to the pellets they're practically inhaling off his palm.

"I got this one house I'm working on right now with an indoor pool," I say, although mansion is probably a better word for it.

"When's it supposed to be finished?" Marc asks.

"Next year." *If we're lucky.* Contractors that can't complete their projects on time are the bane of my existence.

"You should put one in your house," Beck suggests after standing, making me roll my eyes.

"Where? Where would I put an indoor pool?" My house isn't that big. None of ours are. We all live nicely but not extravagantly. At least not in our houses. In our garages? Now, that's a different story.

"You got two bedrooms on your main sitting empty, don't you?"

"Neither are big enough."

"The girls' room is."

The girls. The two sisters we lost last month. Brittni and Makya. It fucking hurts to think about them. It hurts even worse thinking their room will never be filled by them again. I'd never fill their room with anything permanent. Not that Angela would let me.

I jerk a single shake of my head. "It's upstairs."

Brittni and Makya came to us like most of the kids we've fostered over the years, as legal risk placements, but the home they were removed from had a lice infestation so bad the girls had the bugs living on their eyelashes. We never thought their mom would turn things around, and after a while, I think both Angela and I selfishly wished she wouldn't. The girls were skittish, malnourished, and showed up on our doorstep without shoes on their feet. We offered them their own rooms but they only felt comfortable sleeping with each other, so I knocked down the wall separating two of the bedrooms upstairs and made them their own big space. I thought...I *hoped* it'd always be theirs.

But that's the thing about fostering, you have to be prepared to lose the kids at any given time, sometimes without any notice at all. That's how we lost Brittni and Makya. We didn't even get to say goodbye.

Like a goodbye would've helped. I'd still miss them this much whether we had a proper send-off or not. I'd still miss sitting outside their room late into the night, listening to Brittni read out loud to her younger sister until she fell asleep. I'd still miss the overwhelming burst of fabric stiffener whenever Makya entered a room because she sprayed it on every one of her outfits pretending it was perfume. A goodbye wouldn't have done shit to ease this pain.

When you sign up to be a foster parent, all you think about is how you'll be changing the childrens' lives. You never even consider the way the kids will change yours.

"We couldn't fit a real pool in it, but…" Beck doesn't finish, just gets that gleam in his eye that says he's up to something.

I eye him back, the wheels starting to turn inside my own head, too.

"Find the longest hose you got," is all I tell Marc before going over to pick up Jace and carrying him to my car in one arm as I walk backward. The kids turn to watch, sensing the building excitement.

"For?" he asks.

"For a bath," Beck answers.

Blaze tugs on her dad's joggers, then asks him, "Bath?"

Marc shrugs, repeating "Silly" again. We use that word a lot in reference to Funcle Beckett.

Putting Jace down, I say, "Meet at my house in an hour."

CHAPTER 2

Angela

THE DASHBOARD GOES BLACK, BLANKETING ME IN darkness while I mentally prepare myself to go inside the house. The automatic overhead light in the garage already went out a minute or two back.

It feels…different without them. It feels like something's missing. *They are missing.*

It's been a month since the girls were taken from us and placed back with their bio mom. It's been a month since I walked in and heard their voices. It's been a month since I've felt whole.

"Shit," I say between numb lips, hitting the steering wheel with my palm and making a tear fall from my bottom lashes.

This is what we signed up for, I remind myself for what must be the hundredth time in the last thirty days. It's what everybody always says, "*Isn't that the point of fostering, to only keep them temporarily?*"

The point of fostering gets blurred when you fall for every face that comes through your door. The point of fostering gets lost when the children you fall for are returned to homes they had no business being in to begin with. I've loved every kid we've fostered, and some we've seen off to their original families with smiles on our faces. They were watery smiles but they were real because we knew the children were going back to parents that put in the effort. That did the work. That loved their children enough to turn their lives around. Some have been taken from our clutches way before we, or their biological parents honestly, were ready.

Brittni and Makya were. Sisters that came to stay with us at eleven and six with hair so black it was blueish. Thank God too because it made removing the lice from their scalps and eyelids easier. After living under our roof for a year, carving their place in not only our hearts but the rest of our family's, too, the girls were ripped away from us while they were at school, given back to a mom that didn't deserve them the first time around. I'll never forgive myself for not treating that morning, that final goodbye, like it was our last. I didn't know it would be though. I didn't fucking know.

We'd heard of that happening to other foster families, but we never thought it'd happen to us. We never wanted it to happen to us.

My son, Jace, could've been taken from us the same way. We met Jace on the eighth day of his life, still in the hospital, fully dependent on machines. Coty and I took turns staying up for the next thirty after that, helping him through withdrawals from an extremely powerful drug that his body was addicted to before he even left the womb of his birth mother's. The kind of devotion we put in night after night for a complete stranger, the immense love we felt for a baby we didn't create ourselves, there's nothing temporary about that. Lifelong bonds are formed whether you want them to be or not.

We're lucky we were eventually able to adopt Jace because I couldn't have survived losing him.

I'm barely surviving now.

After wiping under both eyes, I grab my bag from the passenger seat.

I need to go inside. I need to see Jace. Hug him and Coty. They make everything better.

They make almost everything better.

The front door shuts a second after the garage door closes behind me. Not a moment later, Marc is climbing our stairs, carrying a wound-up hose.

Blaze trails after him, grasping one of the ends in her small, inquisitive hands, and I stop to cock my head.

A hose?

Coty appears in the kitchen before I can ask any questions, Jace on his back like a monkey. At thirty years old, Coty could still pass as a male model, and the couple gray hairs that've cropped up in that lusciously thick head of unkempt brown hair he has, somehow only make him hotter. It's so unfair.

With no shirt on, he's only in a pair of board shorts, providing the perfect example of just how good he still looks. Rippled muscles down his front and sides all lead to that V disappearing below his shorts that I've become well acquainted with over the last ten years but still find myself wanting to follow. My cheeks burn at the idea of finding the tip to that arrow.

"Hey, babe," Coty greets with a wink that says he knows exactly where my thoughts were headed.

"Hey…" I manage to get out, just as affected by the move as I was when we first met. I'll probably never be desensitized to Coty's winks. He's so damn good at them.

We kiss each other on the lips, then I take Jace from him, squeezing his bare sides until they shake with laughter. For some reason, our son's also in board shorts.

It's a beautiful fall day, full of the brightest hues of orange, yellow, and red this area's capable of—which okay, isn't much—but it's a *cold* beautiful fall day. Not exactly swimming weather.

"You don't mind water, right?"

"Water?" I ask, pulling my lips from Jace's temple while trying not to wrinkle my nose at the smell of unwashed scalp. "Water? Like the kind I work with daily?"

"That's the one." Coty grins, the dimple in his left cheek making its grand entrance. Oh no. I know that dimple. It means utter trouble.

Instead of answering—*it was rhetorical, right?*—I say, "Coty?"

"Yeah?"

"Why are you and Jace wearing swim trunks? Does it have anything to do with Marc and Blaze carrying a hose up our stairs?" This is one of those rare occasions where I hope I'm wrong.

His grin only stretches wider, then Beckett yells from somewhere upstairs, "Are we good?"

Either I missed Beckett's SUV in the driveway when I pulled in, or I was in the garage longer than I thought. I don't know which scenario is worse.

What else have I been missing?

My boyfriend calls over his shoulder, telling his best friend, "We're good!"

"Good for what?" I ask, following him out of the kitchen.

"Here." He turns to grab Jace, then takes the stairs two at a time with me right behind them.

My steps slow when I see the light on in Brittni and Makya's room while my heart speeds up like I'm on the final lap of a marathon.

"What's going on?" comes out in a voice desperately trying to seem even and natural.

I'm desperately trying to seem even and natural.

We pass the bathroom, and seeing Marc inside, fitting the hose to the bathtub faucet with some kind of adapter on the end, I pause.

"Marc? Can you please tell me what's happening right now?" I ask by signing since Blaze is next to him, waving innocently. She may be innocent, but the rest? I've known these knuckleheads long enough to know better. They're doing something I won't like and they almost never ask for permission beforehand. Not when asking for forgiveness afterward is an option.

Marc's usually the voice of reason...when he feels like using it. Coty's most serious counterpart has really settled into his role of husband and father. Not even over time either. It was pretty instantaneous. From day one, he took on Hunter as if Bentlee's son was his own, and nobody'd ever guess Rebel isn't his biological daughter the way he cares for her. One look at Blaze while she's in her daddy's arms, you can tell how good he is with all his kids. He loves each one deeply but equally, and they all know it.

Despite his many responsibilities though, Marc never passes up taking part in his best friends' shenanigans. He's the definition of ride or die. Approaching thirty-two, he still carries the same swagger he did from our Creekwood days. In casual joggers, a gray tee, and a red hat that matches his high-tops, nobody should be able to make such a plain outfit look smoking hot, yet Marc's doing exactly that in my cramped bathroom.

Just like his daughter, he tries playing the innocent card,

too, shrugging with one of his scowls etched on his face. Those scowls don't affect me as much these days, only because now I usually have his wife to decipher them. Since she isn't here at the moment, I'm not sure what this one means, just that it has me worried, especially when the severe expression disappears a second too soon as I'm turning away.

Rushing into the hallway, Terra says, "Aunt Angie," giving me a hug in her…bathing suit? "You're the best."

"Go, go, go," Beckett whispers before Terra's twin brother, wearing a pair of swim trunks as well, hurries from the girls' bedroom to give me an almost identical hug, saying, "I love you, Aunt Angie."

Okay, now I'm really suspicious.

I pat both their heads, asking, "Did your dad put you up to this?" Beckett would absolutely use his kids to butter me up. He's done it before.

The seven-year-olds pull away from my middle, looking at each other with matching guilty looks. *Busted.*

"Oh, neighbor girl, is that you?" I hear Beckett ask from *inside* the girls' room. Inside? What the hell?

His twins and I go into the room that isn't technically the girls' room anymore but still feels like the girls' room; my gaze going straight to the two beds pushed together before I can even notice anything else.

Softly, Coty says, "Angela?"

I tear my eyes away to glance at him. I don't say anything though. I can't. Then he'd know just how bad it's gotten. How bad I've gotten.

"We'll see them again," he whispers, and I try to smile but the act gets lost somewhere from my brain to my lips, all my energy being used to stave off the tears threatening to fall instead. Will we? I'm not so sure. Some parents are happy to let us keep in touch with the kids that've stayed with us, but Brittni and Makya's mom, Nora, was never very friendly to us. Or her daughters.

My shoulders slump and my nose stings. I know exactly how women like Nora operate. I was raised by one.

"Ready?" Marc calls from the bathroom.

Beckett echoes him, asking Coty, "Ready, bro?"

Without taking his mocha-swirl eyes from mine, Coty says, "Ready."

The sound of water running fills the silence, and I finally look around the rest of the room. Taking up the middle of the floor is a rectangular inflatable pool with the other end of the hose draped inside, with Beckett already sitting in it, sporting a pair of colorful board shorts.

"Do I mind water?" I repeat more to myself than anything because water we now have, directly from the bath, filling the kiddie pool with what I'm thinking is warm…

I return my eyes to Coty's. "For Jace?"

He shrugs a shoulder. "It's worth a try."

"No drains," I say with the first grin I've actually felt in a while.

Stepping over the white and turquoise wall, he agrees, "No drains." Slowly, he sits down with Jace in his arms. There usually is a tiny plug for a drain in these types of pools, but judging by where Beckett's ass is currently planted, I'm willing to bet he's sitting directly over top of it to keep Jace from seeing it.

As soon as Jace's feet feel the water, his wide eyes dart around the same way they've done every other time we've tried getting him to take a bath recently. Without a second thought, I follow him and Coty in, work clothes and all, and take our son's face in my hands, promising him, "It's okay. There's nothing that can hurt you."

"And even if there was, we wouldn't let it."

"Beckett," I scold, shooting him an annoyed look. I was just on the verge of letting him off the hook for making his kids shower me with fake affection.

He holds out his gigantic hands, saying, "What? It's true," before telling the twins to get the toys they brought over.

The pool barely fits all six of us, let alone toys, too, but somehow we make it work, squeezing in everyone except for Marc who stands outside the pool, holding Blaze's hands while she stomps in the water, splashing and distracting Jace enough to relax on Coty's lap. Once the pool's about three-quarters full, Marc shuts off the water, then we all play until Paige shows up, looking for her family. Already fully acclimated to these men and their antics, Beckett's better half doesn't even bat an eye at the scene she walks in on, she just gets a stack of towels and dries off her kids. And husband. If there's an opportunity for Beckett to be babied, he'll take it…with a death grip using both hands and a smile from ear to ear that proves he is anything but innocent. Even at thirty-one years old he's still just as incorrigible as he was when we first met. The thin, feathery laugh lines around his eyes are the only sign he's actually matured in the last ten years.

Marc helps Blaze out, then everybody leaves so we can bathe Jace properly, with actual shampoo for his hair.

"How are we going to get all the water *out* of here now?" I ask Coty, using the towel on Jace's tightly curled hair. Our son is sleepy and clean and smells like soap, and I can't keep my smile—my real smile—off my face.

Coty drags the end of the hose from the bathroom into the girls' room, all the way over to the window we opened earlier when the steam got too thick. Sucking on the hose's end until water starts flowing back out, he quickly sticks it out the window to run down the outside of our house, sliding the hose as far as it'll go so the water runs into the grass. He closes the window just enough to fit the hose since it'll probably take a while to drain, then turns to me with his own smile.

"I love you," I tell him, making his smile grow.

Just as quickly that smile falls though, and he busies himself taking Jace from my hold. I know exactly what he's thinking without needing to ask. *I love him but…*

There's always a but for me. *Buts* are the reason I still have my own separate bank accounts. *Buts* keep the door open in case I ever need to make a quick exit. *Buts* are the clause I need in every negotiation so I can pull out whenever I feel the overwhelming need to. When you're born a runner, that urge doesn't just go away. Over time, it lessens, but it doesn't disappear completely. My laces are always tied, maybe not as tightly as they used to be, but they are tied, and every refusal to Coty's many marriage proposals serves as a reminder.

Since we've been serious, I haven't run. I've been right here, side by side with my partner, trudging my way through all the good and the bad. I've wanted to run, several times. I still think about it, even today. When things get hard, that's what I was best at. It was my default setting to save myself.

But what I've learned these past several years of being a foster parent is I'm not the only one I need to protect anymore. It's not all about me. There are bigger, more important, things in life than my feelings getting hurt or my trust being broken. Coty's never broken my trust, not once, and he's never intentionally hurt my feelings.

I'm the one that does that to him by not giving him what he needs to feel secure. I'm the one that's been keeping one foot in the door with my constant buts.

After last month when our world was turned upside down, I'm not sure I feel that need anymore. Not with Coty anyway. He's my Accra, capitol of Ghana—the center of the earth. The rest of my world can flip but Coty will still be at the center of it. He will *always* be at the center of it.

While he puts Jace to bed, I clean up, then I go up behind him when he's brushing his teeth, propping my chin on his bare shoulder blade. We're both wearing dry clothes now, me in a matching pajama set while he's only in a pair of shorts. Shirtless has always been a good look on him, not only because of his sculpted muscles I'll never grow tired of exploring, but because of the meaningful ink decorating his chest.

Staring at him through the mirror, I whisper, "Ask me."

With a mouth full of white foam, he mumbles out, "What?" around his toothbrush.

Not blinking, I repeat myself, telling him, "Ask me." There's only one question he's ever asked me that I didn't have an answer for. Now I do.

His back tenses against my front, but he finishes brushing, spits and rinses, then wipes his mouth on a hand towel before turning to face me, his hand on the counter behind him as he leans against it.

We study each other for a while, I don't know how long exactly, just that it'll never be long enough. No amount of time with Coty will be.

Bending to one knee slowly, cautiously, he looks up at me,

those chocolate eyes so full—full of love, of patience, of perseverance. I don't know what he sees in mine gazing down at him but I hope it's the assurance and gratitude and absolute adoration I have for him.

"Are you sure?"

From the very beginning, Coty told me he'd wait, and he has. He's waited for me to be ready in everything we do together.

My hands find the back of his head, my nails teasing his hairline, not because I need to, but because I want to. My hands are always restless, as unsure as my insides usually are, but right now I am sure, more sure than I've ever been.

I'm ready.

"Ask me," I say again.

"Will you marry me?"

"Yes," comes out so much easier than I thought possible, because with Coty, most things are. I'm the one that makes everything harder. Me and my issues. My past feels like a third person in this relationship most days, just as reliable as Coty, ten times more obstinate. It's always near, waiting for its shining moment to remind me of every insecurity I've ever had.

"Really?" Coty asks, tilting his head to the side. "Because I've been asking—"

"Yes, really. I want to marry you and be your wife—"

"My *wife?*"

With a nod, I drop my arms to his muscular shoulders.

"Fuck, I like the sound of that. Say it again."

I don't hesitate, telling him honestly, "I want to be your wife."

Pushing off the tile floor suddenly, Coty lifts me by my

hips, and carries me straight into our room, right up to the foot of our bed where he deposits me gently.

Immediately coming down on top of me, he asks, "When?"

"Whenever we get married…"

He pretends to think about it, then shakes his head, saying, "Yeah, that doesn't really work for me. I need a specific day."

"Day?" Not month? *Or year?*

Coty doesn't blink, only looks at me expectantly.

Some of those insecurities pop up like gophers in an abandoned field, but I make myself look away from them. I've seen them all before, know them intimately, and I've made Coty wait long enough to succumb to them yet again.

"So…soon?"

"The sooner the better."

"How soon are we talking?" Doesn't it take time to plan a wedding?

A wedding. With guests staring at us. Staring at me.

My nails dig into Coty's neck to keep from tangling together—this time out of need—and he arches into me, settling himself snugly between my spread thighs.

"Now," he says, dropping his mouth to mine and shoving his tongue right in to lick every inch.

His thick cock rubs against my pussy through our shorts until I have to break from the kiss to catch a breath.

"Now isn't a good time," I practically pant out.

"Are you busy?" he asks, tugging my sleep shorts down to my ankles, then pausing to run his gaze over my naked lower half.

I remove my shirt while kicking my shorts the rest of the way off. "Kinda busy."

"This weekend?"

His eyes rise to mine, and at the same time, we both grin, saying, "Fall Fest."

"Next weekend?"

I shrug both shoulders, not committing either way, only watching him closely as I bend my knees again, letting them fall out to the sides.

One single curse leaves his lips before he's on me, licking up my slit, making me hiss on a back arch.

"Is that a yes?" he lifts his head to ask.

"Can we talk about this later? I like what your mouth was just doing better."

"This?" He licks one long, flat-tongued swipe up my pussy, ending at my clit to kiss it sloppily, hungrily.

"Yes," I moan, gripping his hair to keep him there. "That."

Coty shakes free of my hands though, pulling back to say, "Next weekend."

My fists hit the mattress and I lift up on to my elbows, glaring at my infuriating boyfriend between my thighs.

Fiancé?

Fiancé. I officially have a fiancé. A fiancé who's in full negotiation-mode while I'm…horny.

"One week? Is that even enough time to get a marriage license?"

"I'll pay extra to have it expedited."

"But—"

"We've had time, Angela. I'm ready to be married and nothing's going to stop me now that you are, too."

"How do you always know the right thing to say?"

"It's a talent. Set a date and I'll show you one of my others." The promise in his eye causes a tingle to run up my spine, and I visibly shiver, my core aching desperately for his touch again.

"Only one?" I question like I don't already know how talented the man is, then flop back on the bed, huffing in faux boredom. I may even study a nail or two.

I'm flipped over on to my stomach so fast I don't even get a full laugh out before I'm yanked up to my hands and knees.

I hear a muttered, "Brat," behind me, and have to hide a smirk by biting my own shoulder.

Coty runs his palm up my spine, then drags two fingertips down the same path, all the way to my tailbone, over my spread ass crack, before twisting his wrist and driving those same fingers into my wet pussy.

"Next. Weekend," Coty grits while working me over with his fingers, plunging into me over and over again until I'm rocking backward to meet each thrust.

I release my teeth from my shoulder to accuse, "You fight dirty."

"Always have, always will," he rasps against an ass cheek as he lowers his mouth to my opening. I feel him relocate his fingers to my clit, swirling around the sensitive nub, then hear his groan before he latches on to my pussy lips, sucking them from behind.

Holy shit.

I drop my forehead to the comforter, sending my entire back end higher in the air for him, hoping he'll take pity on me and just devour me whole because this seems like the perfect way to go. Face down, ass up, at least I'll die with a satisfied smile.

"Tell me," he has the audacity to demand right now.

My hands twisting by my head, I whisper-shout back, "Coty!"

Air replaces his mouth and fingers, and no, I want him back. All of him.

"Promise me." His shorts hitting the floor punctuate his words as he makes his way over to his nightstand, opening and closing one of the two drawers quickly.

What's he getting? I know it's not a condom because we haven't used one for years. My birth control negates the need. Plus, condoms stink, like literally. Not even his spicy coconut body wash can mask condom odor.

The mattress shifts from him climbing on behind me.

"Promise me and I'll fuck you now."

Lifting my head up, I hook a heel around his hip, nudging his ass to bring him forward so the head of his straining cock is pressed against my pussy, then, and only then, do I ask, "What about next month?" because I fight just as dirty.

"Fuck, Angela," he breathes out, leaning over my back to catch my lips in a rough kiss.

Our mouths busy devouring each other, Coty guides one of my hands to my pussy, dragging three of my fingers through my own wetness. His cock teases both my knuckles and my lips as he glides along my slit—not in, just on—making my whole body quake with anticipation. Fingers aren't enough, especially not mine. There's only one thing that can satiate this urge, and that's Coty. My fiancé. My future husband.

I break from his lips, gasping, "Next weekend."

All at once Coty's hand and cock disappear.

"What—"

I'm quickly flipped on to my back again, looking up at my tormentor smiling so seductively at me, I almost confess my sins—past, present, and future—just to get to the punishment already.

His eyes on mine, he takes my hand still glazed with my own desire, and puts it to his lips, sucking the pointer and middle fingers first, then the ring finger, keeping it in his mouth a little longer as his cheeks hollow out sucking all the way up to the base knuckle. As his lips slide back down the digit, a sparkling platinum ring is revealed.

I look from the solitaire round-cut diamond to Coty and back again.

"You had that next to our bed?"

He nods.

"For how long?"

"However long it took for you to be ready."

Tears fill my eyes and I open my mouth to tell him how sorry I am for being…well, me, but get cut off.

"Angela Taylor, will you make me the happiest man to ever walk this planet by marrying me next weekend and becoming my wife?"

I nod, freeing several tears.

"I promise."

He pushes his cock into my pussy at the same time his mouth lowers to mine, then he's rolling us so I'm on top, looking down at him as I sit up.

Gazing up at me, he wipes my face dry.

"You're so fucking beautiful."

I rock my hips, telling him, "You're just trying to marry me."

"I've been trying for ten years. Now I'm fucking doing it." He lifts his hips off the bed. "Wife."

A moan spills from my lips just before the word "Again" does.

Another thrust from below as Coty possessively growls, "Wife."

"Crap, that's hotter than I thought it'd be."

"How hot?" he asks, propping himself up on an elbow, and deepening his fit inside me.

"Try it again and find out."

He rolls his hips to match mine, saying, "Wife."

My head falls back between my shoulders while I work to keep the pace for us, slow but intentional, like one of those mechanic bulls set to the lowest possible setting. The sexy setting, the one everyone in the club gets turned on by just from watching it move. His tight abs contract beneath my touch, so I scrape my eyes off the ceiling to run them over Coty's face, noticing the newly formed sheen to it as he watches me ride his cock.

Without so much as blinking, his free hand grips one ass cheek, keeping us connected so tightly each rotation massages my clit with his base with absolutely zero let-up. He's. All. I. Feel.

"Jeee-sus," I pant, feeling tremors in my thighs as I clench Coty's middle.

"*My* wife."

"*My* husband."

The eye contact, the terms of endearment neither of us have ever used for anyone else before, not even each other, the complete connectivity—it all stimulates me, *overstimu- lates* me really, in the best way possible, and my jaw drops in a scream from my orgasm unfurling inside me hard and fast. Coty's hand shoots up to pull my head to his as he drinks the sound straight from my lips, my entire body convulsing from the intensity.

"I'm going," he murmurs into my mouth a second before a hot surge erupts from his buried cock, coating my inner walls.

Coty reclines all the way, taking me with him. Slick and spent, I collapse on top of him, my ear to his rambunctious heart, right between his tattoos.

"Where're you going?" I tease when my voice is back.

"To heaven."

"Take me with you."

Against my temple, he whispers, "You're my heaven."

Coty's my home and I'm his heaven. Different terms for different people but they still mean the same thing. Like husband and wife.

Wife.

Of all the names I've been called, wife might be my favorite, only because Coty's name will be in front of it.

Coty's wife. I'll finally be somebody's—somebody that actually wants me.

CHAPTER 3

Coty

"WHO'S THAT?" I ASK, EYEING THE HIGH-school-age girl next to Hunter. Whoever she is, she's *very* interested in whatever my nephew's explaining to her as he bends down next to one of his prized goats.

Marc's already staring at his boy from across the building, his arms crossed over his chest as he grunts one word: "Trouble."

Good for him. It's about time Hunter found himself some trouble. And a girlfriend truthfully. The only girl I've ever seen around him that was even close to his age is Rebel, but that was before puberty hit. They kind of avoid each other these days. That or Rebel's just too damn busy to bother with him.

"How do you know *she's* trouble?" Angela asks, her hackles rising rapidly in defense of a fellow female. She doesn't have to know them to be offended on their behalf, just that there's a patriarchy that needs taken down, and since she's always prepped for battle, she'll happily do it alone.

"I never said she was the trouble." Marc shakes his head, leaving it at that.

Angela looks to me and I shrug. *I don't fucking know.* All I do know is Hunter's never taken a step out of line in his life and probably never will. He's the kindest, gentlest person in the world.

We head back out into the fresh air, exchanging the smell

of hay, fur, and shit for fried dough, warmed sugar, and burning rubber. *Travelling carnivals.* The Fall Fest isn't just about animals, it also has a full farmer's market for local vendors along with a massive carnival. As soon as the sun goes down, shit gets crazy with the younger crowd, so we usually leave before dinner even hits. Our kids enjoy some of the smaller rides and a few games, but they don't need to be here when the teens start drinking, smoking, fighting…and who knows what else. Technically, I do know what else because I used to take part in all of it.

"Is Rebel coming later?" I ask Marc, hoping to God she's not. Marc, Beck, and I would fucking maim a motherfucker. The girl's only fourteen.

"She's already here somewhere."

"She is?" And she's not with us? With the exception of the baby of the group—Angela—most of us are only in our early thirties. How the fuck are we too old and boring for Rebel already?

"She'll make herself known," is all he says on the matter because, as usual, Marc doesn't expand any further than the basics, content to remain as enigmatic as ever.

The three of us meander around on the hunt for the rest of our crew until we find them already aboard the carousel, then we stand at the ride's fence, watching their smiling faces. Jace waves at us every time he passes, Bentlee standing between his horse and Blaze's with a hand on each kid. Terra and Harley are riding the horses behind them, with Paige between her twins. And…yup, Beck is pulling up the rear of the family, riding his very own horse.

Chuckling, I glance at Angela, but she doesn't seem to notice. She's facing the carousel but her eyes are glossed over, like she isn't really seeing it. Almost like she's lost in a day-dream. She's so pretty, not only today but every day. Under her baseball cap, her hair's straight and shiny down her chest. It's gotten darker lately, all that sun damage from working out-doors long gone now that she remains mostly indoors at both Pop The Hood locations. Whenever she's off the clock, she still dresses just as sporty as she did when she was a teenager. Today she's rocking moto-style leggings that disappear into a pair of all-black Adidas Superstars. She's also wearing one of my hoodies. I've always loved her in my clothes. It satisfies some primal instinct in me to claim her publicly.

At the sound of Jace's voice, Angela automatically lifts a hand, the sunlight hitting the new rock on her ring fin-ger, making it shimmer. The image has my heart swelling against my ribs. Now there's no mistaking who she belongs to. Angela is all mine...*almost*. This time next week she'll fi-nally be my wife.

My.

Wife.

I knew it would happen one day. Luckily, a decade with Angela hasn't felt like a decade. When I look at her, I still see the same girl who almost knocked down our door for being too loud on a Friday night. We've been through a lot since then, but I wouldn't trade a second of it because every step we took led us here, and I like here. A lot.

Bentlee's raised voice hits our ears before waning to an echo from passing by in a blur. It's easy to make out what she said: Marc. The hard part is figuring out what it means. There's usually a difference in pitch that tells me exactly what Angela needs when she calls my name, but I'm not as tuned in to Bentlee's frequencies.

We wait until the next rotation, seeing Beck already off his horse and by her side, checking on her and the kids. Bentlee sticks a hand out, pointing behind us.

Marc immediately spins on his heel, darting away, and I turn to follow, latching on to Angela's hand to pull her along behind me. I don't know what's going on and I don't want her out of my sight while I figure it out. Beck's got the others but I can't leave Angela alone. I mean, I *could*—Angela's more than capable of handling herself—but I don't want to. I never want to be anywhere she's not.

Pushing through the tightly packed crowd, we come to a large clearing made by everyone forming a circle—a circle around Rebel holding a girl in a headlock.

Rebel's small for her age…heightwise. In every other way, she fucking towers. She's got Marc's confidence *and* the skills to match.

In the next breath, Rebel tosses the other girl on the ground, revealing her identity. She's the one that was just talking to Hunter.

What the fuck?

Next to me, something snags Angela's attention and she whips her head to the side, ducking around like she's searching for something. Or someone.

Following her gaze, I can't make out anything past the wall of onlookers, so I let go of her hand to wrap my arm around her middle, tucking her into my side.

"Rebel!" Marc barks, finally pulling Rebel's glare away from the girl she's standing over. I can see in her eyes she wants to go another round. But why? What'd this girl do to her?

Rebel straightens, her pale blonde hair blowing around her face and shoulders, and rolls her eyes at her dad. It's a ballsy move—rolling her eyes at Marc Vega—one anybody with even a shred of survival instinct would think twice before attempting. I've seen Rebel do it more times than I can count though. She doesn't just step out of line, she zigzags over it. She's truly fearless. Bending over, she says one last thing to the girl on the ground that we can't hear before disappearing into the crowd.

Beck comes thundering into the clearing, asking, "Yo, who we killin'?" while Angela shakes her head at him, leaving us to go help the girl still sprawled on the ground.

"What?" he asks. "Is that not the vibe?"

"When has murder ever been our vibe?"

"How far back you need me to go? There's Tony, Jason, River, Chaz, Shawnathon." He pauses to spit because fuck Chaz and Shawnathon, then continues, "Those assholes that groped the girls up at the festival. If we're talking more recent, there was that guy that told Bentlee she had a nice ass at the beach this summer. Or at the races, when literally *any* motherfucker gets too close to Paige."

"Alright, you made your point." He's gonna get us pissed off all over again.

Of course Beck has to keep going. "Oh, and that one shitstain at last year's Fall Fest that asked Angie what else she was good at stuffing her mouth with after she beat him in the pie-eating contest."

My back fills with tension and my knuckles ache as I flex them at my sides.

Noticing my sudden change, Beck holds his arms up in a W, all cocky and shit. "Anytime someone wrongs our women, murder's the fuckin' vibe, bro."

Marc jerks a nod with an unapologetic shrug to match.

With a single punch, I put an end to that guy's eating competition career for good. It also jeopardized my family, my livelihood, and my freedom because I could've wound up in jail.

Beck's right. I put Angela above everything, even myself.

But I'd do it all again if I had to. She's my soulmate. There is no me without her, not anymore.

"Well, it wasn't our women getting harassed this time," I inform Beck, my eyes on my future wife while I try to rein in my anger at the memory of that day.

Instead of returning to me when the girl's back on her feet, Angela rolls on to her tiptoes, trying to see above people's heads.

Who's she looking for?

Probably Rebel. We've spent a lot of time with Rebel since meeting her; it's only natural for Angela to worry about her.

But that's not who caught her eye the first time.

Angela knows a lot of people. We all do. Between all of us, we've got three businesses—not to mention Paige's job as a nurse—which have accumulated a lot of contacts over the years. We can't go anywhere without bumping into someone that recognizes at least one of us, so it could be anyone.

Unfortunately in Angela's case, they're mostly men. Women go through her wash, too, but usually it's just the men who form...attachments. Crushes, whatever. It used to piss me off when I worked there, and that was when I was by her side every day, making my presence known. Nowadays, I'm not around as much. Some people might get it in their heads Angela's more available than she actually is.

I shake the thought from mine before it can grow a pair of legs to stand on. Motherfuckers can crush all they want. Angela wouldn't cheat on me. She has no reason to. Like I told Jace, she has everything she could ever want in the life we share together.

"What was it then?"

"Oh, Rebel," I tell Beck with a lift of my hand in the direction Rebel disappeared. "She bodychecked Hunter's…friend."

"Another one?" Beck guffaws. "Dude's never gettin' a girlfriend."

I frown. I knew Rebel didn't back down from anybody, but I didn't realize there was any correlation to who she was fighting. Today's the first time I've even seen Hunter with another girl.

Maybe there's a reason for that.

Maybe Rebel is the reason.

"We thought it'd stop once they went to different schools but this is her third fight this month. All with high schoolers."

Marc, Beck, and I exchange glances, none of us voicing the thoughts we all gotta be thinking.

Hunter and Rebel have been close since they met, and they share the same adoptive dad, but the two are not related in any sense whatsoever. They didn't even grow up in the same house, only the same—large—property that Marc owns.

"Christ," Marc finally mutters. "I gotta tell her mom." He turns away to call Karina. Since Rebel's not racing this weekend, Karina went out of town for a couple nights with her girlfriend. They've been together for a little over a year now and Karina's never been happier. She practically glows nowadays. It's a far stretch from her time at Creekwood. Even when she and Rebel stayed with us for a while, Karina wasn't as happy as she is now. Now she's safe. Completely safe. Her mind, her body, her daughter, *and* her heart…she's found the right people to trust them with, and that can make all the difference.

It's something we've picked up on from fostering: how much personal safety affects not just mental health but a person's overall wellbeing. We've had kids that were sleep-deprived because they didn't feel safe in other foster homes they'd just come from. How can a kid function in school if they're not sleeping? How can they function at all? They can't. They don't. I'd guess it's one of the top reasons for behavioral issues in children, if not the top reason. Their appetites were just as messed up and sometimes it'd take a kid a solid week to finally be able to eat a full meal at our house because their stomachs weren't used to it.

If it weren't for state regulations, we'd foster fifty kids at a time. There are so fucking many—too fucking many—that need safety, and my family and I got plenty to share. True strength doesn't come from self-preservation; it comes from protecting those that can't protect themselves.

Not having any foster kids in our home right now feels wrong, like we're wasting time, like we're missing out on a chance to help someone who needs it. But that's how it goes. Sometimes we have a houseful, sometimes we don't.

"How was she?" I ask Angela, going over to stand beside her.

Her eyes fly to mine. "Who?"

"The girl our niece just pummeled."

"Fine. Embarrassed more than anything." She gestures around at the thinning-out audience, her own face flushing from having so many eyes on her at once.

"Right… So about the wedding…" Because if there's one thing Angela's hated from day one, it's attention, especially in large doses.

"I haven't changed my mind," she rushes out, making me smile.

"Glad to hear it. But I think we should talk a little more about the details."

"Whatever you want." She waves a hand, glancing around again. "I know this is important to you."

To me? This should be important to both of us. It's our fucking wedding. Our *only* wedding. One shot to get it right, to get it perfect, that's it.

"What's that supposed to mean? Is it not important to you?"

She finally looks at me, really looks at me, her hazel eyes softening as she takes my face in her hands to press a kiss to my lips.

"You're important to me, but napkins, centerpieces, place cards, seating arrangements, salmon or chicken, napkins… none of that's important to me."

I laugh against her mouth. "You said napkins twice."

"All I need is you, Jace, the rest of our family, and like three kinds of cake."

"See? I need your help deciding which flavors." I don't really care about all that other shit either but we don't have much of a choice right now. We were only able to find one venue on such short notice, so everything's been expedited to fit our shortened schedule, giving us only hours to make major decisions instead of the typical months, or weeks, or even days most wedding-planning couples get. We had to do a tasting for dinner options yesterday, and we're meeting again tomorrow to go over alternatives for flower arrangements. Angela fucking hates flowers, almost as much as attention, but every wedding needs *something* to decorate with apparently, so the venue's on-site planner is making us choose another theme. Or whatever. I don't really get why we need a theme, or color scheme. Can't we just say our vows, then party? We're pretty good at it.

Actually we don't really party at all anymore, except for the kids' birthdays, then we go all out.

I should've stolen Angela away the moment she agreed to marry me so we could elope. Then it'd be done already, with none of this extra stress.

That's what this is, right? Wedding jitters?

Wedding jitters I can deal with. My résumé running companies shows that. I make important decisions all day, every day, but I don't want to have to plan this wedding by myself. In addition to right now being an incredibly busy time for me professionally, I'd prefer we plan one of the biggest days of our lives together. That way it's ours, instead of just mine.

If I have to, I can take the lead on this wedding…as long as that's all this is. Because marriage jitters, that's a different story entirely.

She's not having second thoughts about *me*, is she?

That thought from before springs back up.

Admittedly, Angela's been a little off lately—more withdrawn, even spacey at times—but that was before we even got engaged. Since that night, her mood's been fine. Not fine, but better. There's definitely been improvement.

Until now.

I look between her eyes, wanting to see for myself what's troubling my bride, but she closes them, shutting me out. Now what the fuck is that about? Because we don't shut each other out. Not at this stage in the game.

"I love you so much," she whispers like it's painful.

As much as I want to say it back, because I do, I fucking love Angela, I swallow the sentiment. Instead, I make myself ask, "What's wrong?"

"Nothing. I just…" She steps back and scrubs her hands down her face. Dropping them, she looks around before jerking a thumb over her shoulder. "I'm gonna try to find Rebel. See if I can set her straight."

I half-scoff, half-laugh.

The smile she gives me in response is an imposter, a fucking fraud compared to the smiles she usually gives me.

I *know* something is wrong. I can feel it. But I can't make her tell me if she doesn't want to.

So I'll do what I always do when Angela isn't ready, I'll wait.

And pray it's not what my brain keeps hinting at because that I can't handle. Angela knows how I feel about cheating. It's a fucking disgrace of an excuse for being weak. My own father showed me exactly what I don't want to be…and what I don't want to be with—the lying, the sneaking around, the different personalities, hell, the different lifestyles. My dad had a whole other life than what he presented at home with me and my mom.

Since Angela's one of the strongest people I've ever met, I've never had to worry about her cheating. Before. Before she started acting like a stranger.

CHAPTER 4

Angela

P ASSING BY A CORNDOG CART, THE SMELL OF sweet cornbread quickly gets doused by its neighbor's citrusy aroma of freshly squeezed lemons a worker is using to make lemonade. Just across from the food section, it's practically impossible not to spot Rebel along with her two best friends, Emaleigh and Letty. They've completely commandeered the balloon water race stand.

Rebel's standing on the counter, reaching above her head for the biggest teddy bear I've ever seen. Next to her sits Emaleigh, legs crossed tightly under her burnt-orange floral dress while she watches their other friend playing a round solely by herself. Letty's body is convulsing like she's operating a machine gun as she shoots water across all the creepy clowns' faces, barely getting enough water in their somehow creepier mouth-holes to even partially inflate the balloons behind their heads.

When a group of boys around the girls' age tries to take the other guns, Letty turns the water gun on them instead, soaking all five until they run off, leaving a trail of nasty insults in their wake.

Spinning around, Rebel shouts, "Winner!" before dropping the giant teddy into Emaleigh's lap.

Using her finger on the gun's nozzle to spread the

stream into a wide fan, Letty sprays both girls, creating the best kind of laughter to exist.

The pure joy on my niece's face makes the lecture I was about to give her shrivel into a ball small enough to slip back down my throat. It's not like lectures ever get us very far with Rebel anyway.

"Where's the attendant?" I ask instead. There's no way they won that bear fairly.

"Aunt Angela," Rebel greets without making a single move to get down.

After putting the water gun back in its holder, Letty shrugs, and mutters, "He pissed himself."

"No, I didn't!" comes from somewhere behind the wall of clown heads and half-filled balloons.

Oh my God. As much as I hope they didn't tie the attendant up, I wouldn't put it past them.

I turn to Emaleigh. "What happened?"

With a giggle as light as air, she explains, "He hit on me, so Letty sprayed the front of his pants until it looked like he peed. He ran to the back to…I don't know…change probably." Her shrug is an exact replica of the one Letty just gave.

"He hit on you?" I ask before raising my voice to the perv in the back, yelling, "You know these girls are only fourteen!"

"He knows now." Rebel's dark chuckle reminds me of Marc's so much I have to stop myself from laughing, too. "Want one for Jace?" she asks seriously, gesturing to the ceiling of stuffed animals above her.

I shake my head. "Get down before your dad sees you up there and starts asking questions. If Marc, or either of your uncles, finds out a grown man was hitting on you girls..." My eyes widen for effect, then narrow when it actually works.

Even though she's no longer looking at me, Rebel appears downright nervous, and I know her well enough to know she's not afraid of anything, least of all our family members.

"No way. Is that really them?"

Them? My breath freezes in my lungs, turning to blocks of ice.

"Wait, wait, wait," she murmurs before lifting on to her tips of her boots, angling her body for a better view. "Angela, I swear I just saw—"

"Brittni and Makya," I finish for her, more statement than question. I thought I was the only one. I thought I was going crazy. I thought my grief over their absence was making me see their faces in others.

If Rebel is seeing Brittni and Makya, too, then that means they're really here and I might actually have a chance at seeing them again. I've dreamt of this day, agonized over what I'd do, what I would say, and now that I'm here, I have no idea how to act, or what I *should* say. As I've gotten older, I expected to...grow up, I guess, but the truth is how I felt mentally at seventeen is exactly how I feel now, just with more insight. Even after years of adulting, I still feel just as awkward as I always have.

"Where'd they go?" Whether I have a solid plan or not, I'm not missing what might be my only opportunity to see them again.

"I don't know, but they were just standing by the pretzel cart."

"Ordering?"

Rebel's eyes flit down to her friends, lingering on Letty's a second longer than Emaleigh's before she rasps, "No. Just staring at it."

My nose tingles as tears build behind my eyes.

"Okay," I force out, mentally shaking myself. I'm the adult here. I can help. I will help. "Emaleigh, leave the bear here and you—"

"Don't leave the bear."

I stare up at my niece. "Why?"

"She deserves compensation."

"She deserves an apology," I tell the girls, making sure to touch on each of their gazes focused on me. "You're allowed to exist in this world any way you want. You shouldn't get harassed because of it. He owes you an apology, Emaleigh. I'll go back there right now and make sure he gives you one." *Hopefully he's dressed by now.*

Emaleigh pushes to standing, oversized bear still in her clutches, and shakes her head. "I don't want an apology from him. It's not like he'd actually mean it. They never do."

Emaleigh's words ring with a truth every woman knows all too well, but she doesn't sound bitter about it. Just indifferent. She's a very, *very* pretty young girl, and unfortunately, men of all ages have already started taking notice. And apparently, they've had no qualms letting her know it.

Letty was right to drench that asshole.

"Fine. Take the bear." I pull a twenty from my back pocket. "And go buy a couple pretzels while I look for Brittni and Makya."

Rebel grabs two more teddy bears, these only slightly smaller than Emaleigh's, and jumps down, landing in front of me and her friends…and the giant bear. What the hell are they gonna do with all these damn big bears?

"What are those for?" I ask her.

"Not what. Who. They're for Brit and Kya." She hands one over to Letty, and for a moment, I see the sweet little girl Rebel used to be.

Then I remember she's technically stealing.

"One's enough," I tell them, collecting the two smaller ones and tossing both back over the counter. We're already pushing our luck here.

Her gaze on the trampled-over grass between us, Letty murmurs, "If they're staring at the pretzel cart, they could be thirsty, too."

I study Letty, comparing the confident girl I walked up on to this timid one now. She lives further down the canyon from us, in a trailer with her dad. I don't know all the details of her situation, just that Marc doesn't make her pay for anything at Ride It, not even the dirt bike he lets her use after her old one broke down. Actually, now that I think about it, I'm almost positive he bought it for her and just lets her store it there.

I need to talk to Rebel after this and see what else her friend's in need of.

After switching out the bill for my credit card, I give it to Rebel with instructions to get full meals. I don't specify how many in case Brittni and Makya aren't the only ones going hungry.

We head to the pretzel cart, then I leave them in line to search the area. It doesn't take long for me to catch sight of the two girls who lived under my roof for the past year. I follow the sisters, keeping a safe distance while searching near them for anyone that might appear responsible, but come up empty. *Of course.* Nora's not responsible. She wasn't when the girls were taken out of her custody and she's not now. I don't know what she did to convince the court system otherwise but it's obvious it was just a smoke show. With hustlers, it always is.

Nora doesn't even want her daughters, only the added benefits they earn her, like welfare. She shouldn't just get her kids taken away, she should be in jail. In my eyes, she's a criminal. She uses her own flesh and blood as objects, as payouts. Same with the foster parents who do it, too. There are far too many people whose main interest in fostering is the money the state pays them.

Yes, it takes money, at least a little, to raise healthy, stable, happy children, but it also takes fucking willpower, a lot of it; and the only motivation Brittni and Makya's bio mom has is to cash in on as many opportunities as possible while doing next to nothing to earn them. Much like my own mother, she refuses to get an actual job. It'd decrease her benefits after all. She'd rather her daughters eat off the floor than go to work and be able to afford a table.

Seven-year-old Makya turns around and our eyes almost connect but don't before her older sister tugs on her hand, both of them running over to stand in front of a fan, the tangled messes of black hair on their heads barely moving from the wind.

When the sisters came to our house, not only did they have lice on their scalps but also their eyelashes. Their. Eyelashes. And now, today, their hair hasn't been brushed for who knows how long, probably from their mother's house still being fucking infested, and just like before, Nora's refusing to get them treatment.

Shit. It's worse than I thought. They're not just going without a meal, they're going without basic care.

What do I do?

What *can* I do? Call child services? Nora has them fooled. She wouldn't have gotten Brittni and Makya back if she didn't.

The hardest part is I'm not allowed to play judge and jury—that's what the state's supposed to be doing—I'm expected to only offer a temporary solace to those assigned to me.

Temporary.

There's nothing temporary about how I feel standing here, seeing these girls suffering.

I use my thumb fingernail to scrape across every other nail, pushing each cuticle back until they're all red and angry.

And just like that, I'm right back to being a child again, under my own mother's cruel thumb—helpless, hopeless, and just trying to make it to another day.

But I'm not helpless. Not anymore. Now I have the one thing hustlers crave most.

I have it…it just isn't a good time to give it up. Not with a wedding literally days away. A wedding with hand-folded and pressed napkins.

Shit!

That's the difference between a real parent and just someone with kids—the grit, the tenacity, the all-out recklessness that takes over when one of your children is in danger. I would do anything to save the girls.

Anything? Really, truly anything?

My feet carry me forward, my mind racing headfirst into a half-cooked plan.

"Hi, girls," I croak out when I'm standing next to them, trying to keep my tears from falling as I stare into eyes that are helpless, hopeless, and just trying to make it to another day.

Those same eyes staring back at me don't even have eyelashes, most likely from the girls plucking them clean out as their own form of treatment.

Would I do anything to save these girls?

Yes. Really, truly anything.

CHAPTER 5

Angela

"HEY, ANGELA, CAN YOU SIGN FOR THIS?" ONE of our parts delivery drivers asks, holding out a clipboard over a large box that probably has more to do with the garage side of things than my car wash portion. I sign anyway since I'm the boss. One of them. Beckett's at Pop One today, while Tysen and I hold down the fort here at Pop Two. After Coty started his design company and Marc built his own motorsports complex, Beckett and I split Pop The Hood responsibilities pretty much equally. He's at Pop One for the first half of the week while I take care of Pop Two, then we switch for the last half. We have trustworthy, hands-on managers at both locations and sections of the business; but I'll never forget what it was like to work somewhere without an owner ensuring things run a certain way.

"Damn, looks like I missed my chance," the driver says.

At my blank expression, he points at my engagement ring.

"Who's the lucky guy?"

"Coty?" I thought it was common knowledge that we were together. It has been ten years. But some of the newer employees might not be clued in yet since Coty is hardly ever here anymore. I certainly don't act like I'm single though, so I'm not sure why he, or anybody, would think that.

Tysen chuckles as he passes. Walking backward, he teases, "Coty? You're not sure?"

"I'm sure. It's Coty," I bite out much harsher than necessary. It's always been Coty, and as long as he'll still have me, it'll always be Coty.

The driver looks between me and Paige's brother over my shoulder before saying awkwardly, "Well then, congratulations."

I smile so hard my eyes crinkle painfully. *Will Coty still want me after this?*

"You okay, Angela?" Tysen questions from behind me.

Instead of answering, I wave at the box, and say, "Figure out who this belongs to, would you?"

I don't trust myself to answer right now. I have too many balls up in the air to know if I'm okay yet. Every other time I've tried my hand at juggling, I've failed. I cannot fail this time.

My phone rings, and since I've been waiting two hours for a response, I answer it without even checking the name.

"Hello?"

"Hey."

I pause at Coty's voice, letting his familiar tenor wash over me. He's not who I was expecting, yet he's exactly who I needed. That's why it's Coty, why it'll *always* be Coty. I couldn't stop loving him any more than the moon could stop orbiting Earth. Not all pulls are as indestructible, but my pull to Coty was, is, and forever will be.

I escape into my office so I can hear better. We haven't had a chance to talk since yesterday. By the time I got home last night, it was too late, and this morning I left earlier than usual so I could make a phone call without anyone around.

"Are you ready to pick a theme?"

Shit. With everything going on, I forgot about our appointment with the wedding planner this afternoon.

Another ball gets added to the mix.

I trap the phone between my ear and shoulder to grab a stack of forms inside my office, saying, "Um, I thought we'd go with whatever theme you wanted."

"Don't do this."

The papers in my hands fall to the desk silently.

"Do what?"

"Don't make this about me." The uncertainty in his voice buckles my knees and I fall into my chair. "Because if it's only about me and what I want, then you can walk away."

"I can't. I won't," I promise him. I hate that he still has to worry about me running. I hate that I still justify that worry.

"What happened yesterday? You said you were checking on Rebel."

"I did."

"But that's not all you did," he says thickly. "You took the Jeep. For what?"

"Something came up."

I didn't return to Coty right away. I didn't return to him until late last night when he was already home. After I approached Brittni and Makya, I stayed with them until Rebel and her friends brought over the food I had them buy, then I stayed even longer, making sure they ate it all.

Since the only thing free about the Fall Fest is attending it, Nora told the girls they could go…without her. They told me they wanted to go because they knew our family would be there. They wanted to see us. They wanted to see me. So using loose change they found between couch cushions, they caught the transit. I couldn't let them take it back. I didn't want them to go back at all. I texted Paige and asked if she could take Coty and Jace home for me, allowing me to return

Brittni and Makya to Nora's. If I hadn't, Nora could've called the cops, or worse DCFS, then *I* would've been in trouble.

I struggled with that decision all night, but after spending this morning on the phone with Beckett's attorney father, Marshall Meyers, he convinced me I made the right choice. Keeping this private is my best option.

"Business?" Coty asks with an edge to his voice I've never heard before. It's almost accusatory. "I thought your business was my business."

"It is, but…"

On a sigh, I drop my head back and inspect the ceiling, seeing all the cracks I usually don't even notice because I'm too busy. Then I lift my left hand, studying my ring instead, specifically the diamond's perimeter. Around and around and around, no end in sight.

"Do you ever feel like you're just going in circles? Like nothing is really changing. Everything around you changes. Just…not you."

After a long pause, Coty asks, "Did I do something?" and I shake my head even though he can't see me.

"No, not you as in *you*, you as in a general you. Someone can do all these things, make all these strides, but ultimately, they end up back where they started."

"Like a roundabout?"

A ghost of a smile touches my lips. "Sure. Like a roundabout."

"I think…that if we're talking about a roundabout…there are still ways to get out. Whether it's one or multiple other paths, a person can always choose another way to take, it's just up to them when and which one."

"And if it's not a roundabout? If there are no other ways out?"

"Then you stop."

"Stop?"

"You stop the fucking cycle yourself," he says. "You did it with your mom. You're nothing like her. You're patient and selfless and thoughtful. You're the best fucking mom to...Jace."

His hesitation before our child's name nearly kills me as I stifle a sob in my throat. That list should be longer. It could be longer. I'm working on making it longer.

"You didn't just stop that cycle, Angela, you fucking smashed it. I'm lucky. I'm marrying a woman who accomplishes anything she puts her mind to."

"Are you?"

Coty doesn't answer right away, then quietly, he asks, "Am I?"

I was referring to the part about the woman who accomplishes anything she puts her mind to but it feels like he's referring to another part.

"One of the new hires saw my ring today and said you were lucky," I joke.

He lets out a strange sort of chuckle at the same time a text comes in. I pull my phone away from my ear to read it, and end up missing whatever he says next.

I read the message again, giving my own strangled laugh at the audacity.

She wants more.

Of course she does. After all, where there's smoke there's fire.

But if one log gets pulled from this fire, the whole thing

could cave in, leaving two innocent lives in the ashes. I have to be careful.

I don't feel very careful when I imagine Brittni and Makya inside the house I delivered them to last night. I feel reckless, the same recklessness I felt back at Creekwood when I didn't want my mom to get her claws into the boys across the hall because I loved them.

I smashed the cycle with my mom but not the cycle within myself. I've worked tirelessly to not become my mother. I've been at war with myself for as long as I can remember, constantly fighting against any instinct that pops up trying to make me *her*. I can't say I've put in the same effort to question what makes me *me*. If I had, I wouldn't still be this scared little girl pretending to be something she's not. I wouldn't be here, ten years later, in another predicament where I keep secrets from Coty all over again. I am still stuck in my own roundabout. I recognize the paths laid out before me because I've already faced them. I know exactly which one's harder and which one's easier. Having Coty by my side is almost always easier for both of us. But this time it's not. The easier path for me is the harder one for him. That's why I'm not choosing it.

I love Brittni and Makya and I'll do anything to protect them. If anyone should be able to understand that, it's Coty. He fucking *fights* for his family regardless of the consequences.

When the smoke clears from all this, I pray he'll still want to.

"Cars."

"What?"

"Cars. That can be our theme."

I can hear the shake of his head as he says, "Everything in our life revolves around cars."

"Exactly, it's the perfect theme for us."

"How—"

"I'll call the planner and explain everything so we don't have to meet again," I say. "And that bakery you wanted us to try out…how about I do that myself, too? I'll pick the cake flavors."

"The flavors?"

"All three," I remind him, feeling my armpits sting from the sudden sweat attack.

"Are you sure?"

"Mmhmm," I mumble so I don't have to lie any more than I already have.

Neither of us speaks for a minute, and I picture him with that unkempt brown hair of his, along with those eyes I love so damn much. If he were here right now, looking at me with them, I don't know if I could do this.

I don't know if I can, period.

That's not going to keep me from trying though.

"Coty?"

"Yeah?"

"I'm the lucky one," I say, resolute, because of that I am sure. No matter what happens, I'm lucky to have met Coty, to have loved Coty, to have been loved by Coty.

I hang up before he can say anything else, then send out the quickest text I've ever typed.

Amount?

There may be fire where there's smoke, but without oxygen to fan the embers, the flames will die out. To do that, I need to cut off her air.

CHAPTER 6

Coty

M Y PHONE BUZZES IN MY POCKET AGAIN. IT'S always fucking buzzing. There isn't a day that goes by where there isn't at least one "emergency" on at least one of my build sites, and today I've got crews at six.

I'm fortunate to have so many clients, but it can be a lot sometimes, like when I'm trying to get married. We haven't even talked about a honeymoon yet, but damn could I use one. One without any housing material, or permits, or inspections, or phone calls every thirty seconds from people asking questions I already answered; just sand and sun and maybe a cocktail or two. Yeah, some alone time on a beach with my new wife sounds pretty fantastic right about now. If I didn't have so much on my plate, I swear I'd pull a Marc and drive Angela straight to the airport after our reception. We'd choose a destination, any destination, and just go.

We'll honeymoon eventually. We got the money for it, it's just a matter of making time.

Up ahead Pop Two comes into view, so I veer into the right lane. As I'm pulling in, I spot both Beck's and Marc's bikes already parked in the lot. We still try to get a ride in every now and then, but they didn't say shit to me about fitting one in today.

Not that I would've taken them up on it anyway. I'm only here to see Angela.

And all the new faces working alongside her every day.

I meet my boys at the bay they're in, glancing around and asking them, "My fiancée around here somewhere?"

They both shake their heads.

Beck speaks first, eyeing me as he says, "Jeep's not here."

Yeah, I noticed that, too, but after Angela shared that fun story yesterday about a new hire admiring her engagement ring, I offered to take her to lunch today, so she knew I'd be coming by. She didn't say anything in response though…so maybe she didn't hear me.

Regardless, today's Tuesday. She works at Pop Two on Tuesdays. Unless she and Beck switched up their schedules without telling anyone to keep all the employees on their toes, which they've been known to do occasionally. Although, she usually tells me.

She usually tells me everything.

"Did she go over to Pop One?"

"Nah, I was there all morning and didn't see her. I just stopped over here during my lunch because this guy needs my help." He jerks a thumb at Marc.

Marc's head is already shaking. "I don't need help."

Beck scoffs and I force out a laugh.

While they argue, I pull my phone out, scrolling through my texts first. None are from Angela, but there is a vague one from the wedding venue's planner asking me to return her phone call as soon as possible to let her know how we'd like to proceed. I click on my voicemails, lifting the phone to listen to hers specifically out of the five new ones awaiting my attention. Proceed? What does that mean?

"Hello, Mr. Walsh, I was hoping to follow up with Ms. Taylor directly, but I can't seem to get ahold of her. Following our conversation yesterday, I spoke with my manager, and got some clarification regarding the questions y'all had. We understand things happen, unexpected expenses arise, feelings change. Your situation is unique in that we haven't had time to prepare in advance like we normally would, and so the only money that's been paid is your initial deposit. With that said, in the event that your wedding is cancelled, we would not require the full amount of your bill. I know that was Ms. Taylor's main concern. However, you would forfeit the deposit entirely. Now, if you were to reschedule the date, your deposit could be put toward your new date—"

My ears fill with my heartbeat until I can't even hear the wedding planner over it.

Cancelled? Rescheduled? What the fuck?

With shaky fingers, I exit out of voicemails, quickly scanning my missed calls and emails. So many notifications, but not one with Angela's name on it.

"Ty?" I call out, my eyes still on my phone. "Do you know where Angela might be?"

"I assumed with you."

I look up, meeting Ty's gaze dead-on. Do I really need to point out that she clearly is not with me? I wouldn't fucking be asking if she was.

Beck's brother-in-law glances at Beck, Marc, then me, and I have to clench my phone in my fist to keep from throwing it.

"She was only here for a few minutes this morning. After getting something out of her office, she left again, saying she had an appointment that might take all day." He shrugs like he's sorry.

Turning away, I tap Angela's name and bring my phone back up to my ear. It goes straight to her voicemail, so I hang up before trying again.

If the wedding planner was trying to get ahold of us to ask how we wanted to proceed, that means the wedding wasn't cancelled...yet.

Is that what Angela wants? To cancel the wedding? Our fucking wedding. Why else would she ask about it?

Yesterday, Angela offered to tell the planner our theme, but she didn't. She also offered to order the cakes. Did she even do that?

After a quick search, I dial the bakery we discussed using.

"Yes, hello," I say when I finally get a person on the line and not an automated recording. "My fiancée was in there yesterday to place an order for a few wedding cakes for this weekend." I nod along, telling the guy which name to look up.

The silence around me builds like a cacophony of pissed-off cicadas, forcing me to glance up and check my surroundings. Is she here?

Still no Angela in sight.

Fuck.

On both sides of me, Beck and Marc regard me with what looks like sympathy but feels like shit. Mainly because I know that look. I *hate* that look. It's a mix of pity and suspicion with a heavy dose of judgment. It's the same look my mom would get from people whenever they'd ask about my father's work as a professor, and why, if his classes were held on weekdays, during the day, was he always putting in nights and weekends, too? Unfortunately, most teachers do end up putting in a lot of hours outside of their regular workday, but my dad's not one of them. His nights and weekends are spent with his students, just not to work on their poetry.

That's not what's going on here though.

It's not. My dad's a cheater and Angela's not. She wouldn't do that to me. Couldn't. I'd notice.

Wouldn't I?

This is just…a misunderstanding.

"No Angela Taylor, huh?" I say. "What about Coty Walsh?" *Nothing.* "There must be a mistake. Can you try Angela Walsh?"

Mistakes and misunderstandings. That's all this is. Neither of which will stop me from marrying the love of my life. The devil himself could spring up from the underworld, prepared to drag me to hell, and I'd tell him to wait his fucking turn. I got a girl I'm going to marry first. My girl.

"You said she came in yesterday? There was one woman who called in yesterday, asking about our prices for a wedding, it sounded like it was soon, but she didn't place an order."

Nowhere near ready to accept that answer, I immediately hang up and try Angela again.

"You can't get ahold of Angie?" Beck asks.

Focusing solely on my phone, I mumble, "Something came up." That's what she said yesterday. That's the excuse she used.

And it sounds just as bogus coming out of my mouth as it did hers.

"Something? Or…someone?"

I freeze my entire body to glare at Beck, then bite out the only word I'm capable of right now, "What?"

"Brace yourselves, fellas. Fuckery's afoot."

Marc eyes him. "What kind of fuckery?"

Tilting his head to the side, Beck shrugs. "The night of the Fall Fest, someone deactivated the alarm at Pop One. I checked the security footage and you know who I saw?"

"Don't," I warn, my voice dripping with malice.

"Angela."

Marc catches me with his hand on my chest. I don't even know who I'm going for, just that I'm fucking going. I want blood and anyone's will do right now, even my boy's.

"What was she doing?" Marc asks carefully.

"Cleaning the inside of the Jeep."

"Why the fuck wouldn't you just say that? You made it sound like—"

"Like she's fucking around on our boy?"

"That's not what she's doing!" She promised she'd marry me. She fucking promised. Why would she do that if she was fucking around behind my back?

"Then what'd she do after the Fall Fest that required the back seat of her car to be vacuumed and wiped down, then vacuumed and wiped down again? She fucking scrubbed every inch of that seat, bro. I watched it with my own eyes."

The back seat…

My stomach cramps at even the mention of it.

Angela, my fucking Angela, doing…what? Fucking someone back there? Riding him the way she rides me? Trusting him the way she trusts me?

No. I can't. I can't imagine it. I refuse to venture down that plank yet. I need more details before I abandon this ship of sanity I'm fucking clinging to right now.

Is this how my mom feels all the time? Is this why she willingly acts oblivious? Because the pain of betrayal is too much to endure?

She'd have to love my dad the way I love Angela, and there's just no way that's possible. There's no comparison. My mom cherishes her lifestyle enough to sacrifice her marriage for it. I cherish Angela enough to sacrifice my lifestyle for her. We're not, and could never be, the same. Not even fucking close.

I point a finger in Beck's face that he doesn't so much as flinch at, and grit out, "Don't put that shit in my head."

"Fine. Maybe she's not cheating on you."

"She's not," I snarl.

"But she is hiding something."

"She..." I stop short. She is. Angela is keeping something from me, from all of us, and the worst part is I don't even know for how long. She hasn't been herself for a while.

"Why don't you check GPS and see what she's doing?"

"I don't have GPS on Angela. I *trust* her." I do trust Angela—usually.

"Trust isn't not having GPS on someone, it's having GPS on them and never needing to check it," he says.

No words, I just shake my head and step away from Marc's hold. Once in a while Beck surprises us with a pearl of wisdom, but this is not one of them. I know Beck and his wife have GPS on each other's phones, but Angela and I don't. The thought never even crossed my mind because *that* is trust.

"I trust her," I repeat for my sake more than anyone else's. I do need to find her though. I need to look into her eyes and ask her why she's doing whatever it is she's doing.

If that means violating her trust, so be it. She violated mine first by not being honest and...fuck! What happened in that back seat? I want to know as much as I don't.

"Fuck it. How do I—"

"Found neighbor girl," Beck says, cutting me off.

"What? What do you mean you found her? I didn't even give you my phone yet."

"It's already on mine." He flashes us his screen, and sure

enough, there's my fiancée's beautiful, smiling face. The face I've fallen asleep to every night for the past ten years of my life. The face I've woken up to just as many mornings. The face I've kissed every inch of. The face I've memorized enough to know exactly what she's feeling when she's feeling it, not after.

I should've done something sooner. I knew something was off long before today and I didn't intervene. I'm supposed to be faster. I thought I was faster.

I also thought Beck only kept tabs on his own wife, not mine.

Soon-to-be wife.

Is she still my soon-to-be wife?

"Why do you have GPS on Angela?"

"Why do I have GPS on all you motherfuckers? For emergencies."

Marc and I exchange looks. All of us? He has GPS on all of us?

"How'd you get the passcodes?" he asks Beck, and I'm wondering the same fucking thing. Also, when the hell did he have the opportunity to type them in without us noticing? My phone's always on me, and Marc's got two teens, so his ass is on call 24-7.

"Easy. I just went down the list of birthdates in your houses until I got the right one. You use Blaze's," Beck says, pointing at Marc. "Bentlee uses yours. Coty uses Angie's, and Angie uses her own." He shakes his head like he's disappointed in us for not knowing that but it's called fucking respect. I could've guessed that, too, but I didn't.

But maybe I should've? For situations like this.

What even *is* this?

An emergency.

"You don't get to track my wife," Marc growls, pushing into Beck's space now.

I quickly pluck Beck's phone from his hand before any blows can get thrown. They can tear each other's heads off for all I care. I just want to know where Angela is.

"Relax. I already told you, I don't actually check up on anyone. It's just in case shit ever goes down."

Beck tries to rub Marc's nose with his but Marc shoves his jaw away from him, mumbling something about our friend being an asshole.

Yeah, no shit. An asshole who occasionally has his moments.

"Either of you know where this is?" I ask, glaring at the unfamiliar address. Is it a house? I swear to fucking God…

Beck shuffles over for a closer look first. "Oh, shit."

"What?"

"That's my dad's office."

"What does that mean? Why is she at your dad's, Beck?"

"Well… Look, where's Jace, man?"

My head's already rotating on its fucking hinges. No. No. That's not even… She wouldn't. She wouldn't try to take Jace from me. Jace is my family. Our family.

A family I thought Angela was the center of.

"He's with Bentlee today. Wasn't Bentlee at home when you left?" I ask Marc, my chest feeling like it's being loaded with weights. Twenty pounds. Thirty.

"She was, yeah. Want me to check with her?"

"Found Lee-Lee," Beck says, making Marc growl but also lean in at the same time.

"She's…" Beck stops to look up at me. "I can't be sure

'cause she's not coming from the canyon, but it looks like she's headed in the direction of my dad's office."

Forty. Forty fucking pounds and my ribs are about to crack from the pressure. *I'm* about to crack from the pressure.

This can't be happening.

"Marc."

"She wouldn't fucking dare," he pledges, gripping my shoulder.

"But…she is. It fucking shows it right here." I tap Beck's screen with the tiny picture of Bentlee's face moving along the road.

"We don't know that. Goddamn it." He rips the phone from my hand, saying, "That's why this shit's dangerous. We're jumping to conclusions before we know anything."

"Or we're saving our friend from losing his kid." Beck goes over to grab his helmet off his work bench.

"How are we doing that? If Angela's got your dad helping her…"

Marc doesn't need to finish his sentence. We all know my chances going against Beck's dad. Marshall Meyers is the best family attorney in the area. He's been helping our family win custody battles for years. He mopped the fucking floor with both Shawnathon and Chaz.

I can't even believe Marshall would take Angela on as a client. Isn't there some kind of conflict of interest here? I'm not close to Marshall but Beck's practically my brother. Marc, Beck, and I have been best friends since we were kids, riding together, living together, growing together.

Together.

"By being faster," floats past my lips. Together, the three of us are faster. We've always worked better as a unit.

"Than who? B's dad? We don't know the first thing about filing court documents."

"No, Lee-Lee," Beck tells him while looking at me. "We just have to get to her before she gets to Angie."

"I already fucking told you, Bentlee wouldn't..." Marc stops, his gray eyes narrowing at the phone in his grip.

"What is it?"

"Paige. Doesn't she have work today?"

"Yeah, why?"

"Because she's on the move now, too. Same fucking direction."

"That woman loves a good spankin'." Beck puts his helmet over his head, lifting the visor. "Ooh, boys. Now we've got ourselves a fair fight."

"It's not a fight," I tell him, not even convincing myself.

Marc drops his hand by his side and sighs as he shakes his head. "It will be if Angela tries taking Jace from us."

We stare at each other, so much uncertainty sitting between us.

How did we get here? Us versus Angela?

It feels weird even thinking it. Worse than weird. It feels fucking wrong. Suiting up to go against...Angela? My other half? I'd rather shoot myself in the right hand, blow the whole fucking thing to bits, than fight Angela about anything. Literally fucking anything. I don't even argue when she buys the salad mix with the spinach in it, and I fucking hate spinach.

"I'm gonna try calling her again," I say. I have to. Angela *is* us.

"You do that," Beck says. "We'll get a head start."

"Motherfuck." Marc shoves his own helmet over his head.

"Don't go near my wife," he threatens Beck, handing him his phone back. "I'll fucking handle her."

When I hear the voicemail kick on, I hang up. No point in wasting time on a message she'll be hearing straight from my mouth soon enough.

Her and whoever the fuck dirtied her Jeep.

CHAPTER 7

Angela

T HE MEDIATOR GIVES ME A TIGHT SMILE AS WE GET up from the long table. "Congratulations, Ms. Taylor." He sticks his hand out to me.

After staring at the large, weathered palm free of the same sweat that's been coating mine for the last five hours, I wipe my hand on my pants before giving his a shake. *Congratulations.* This doesn't feel like a victory. It does, but not a whole one, not yet. I have to talk to Coty first, because without him…

I have to talk to Coty.

"Thanks," I say, then turn to Marshall, telling him the same thing. This wouldn't have been possible without his help.

"I gotta be honest, she had me nervous there for a bit," Beckett's father says.

I bob my head. "Me, too."

Nora did exactly what I expected her to do, yet still managed to catch me off guard with her ridiculous demands. She didn't just come to play today, she came to win.

And I let her.

I wouldn't have custody of Brittni and Makya if I didn't though, and they're priceless. Their safety is priceless.

Hopefully, Coty sees it that way, too. I need him to because he's my safety.

We take care of payments, then the mediator bids us goodbye, slipping out the door, probably to go do the exact same thing in the conference room just across the hall, minus collect payment because along with mine, I paid Nora's fees, too. It makes my skin crawl imagining him congratulating *her*. She's the one who lost, even though I'm sure she doesn't see it like that.

Alone with Marshall, the man who resembles his son in so many ways except his height, I head for the door, already reaching into my purse for my phone. It's been on silent mode the entire time we've been in here, negotiating the terms and price for the adoption of the girls. Not seeing my engagement ring on my finger makes me pause. It's funny, I've gone almost twenty-nine years without one, but after wearing the ring Coty gave me for less than a week, I'm already used to it. Seeing my hand bare now is…sad.

"Would you prefer to hang out in here for a few? Just until she leaves?" Marshall asks me, before explaining, "Things can be tense afterward."

Automatically, I drop my phone back in my purse and push through the door.

"I'm okay."

I hold my head high as I leave the conference room, making sure I keep my arms glued to my sides so I'm less tempted to use them. After everything the girls told me at the Fall Fest, I want to. What Nora's put those girls through… She's lucky she's walking away at all today.

Nora enters the hallway a moment after I do, instantly scanning me from head to toe, and I fight to keep my hands still.

There's nothing she can use against me, I remind myself. I made sure of it before I stepped into the ring with her today. It's not my first time squaring off against a manipulator. I know what they look for—weaknesses.

That's why I can't even have my phone out right now and risk having her see the model of it. *Where there's smoke there's fire...*

It's all calculations to people like Nora. They don't see people or emotions. They see dollar signs. They see what they want, what they convince themselves they need, and they immediately start scheming on ways to get it. It's obvious in her gaze as it swipes down me again, considering all the opportunities she might've missed out on today.

Oh well. The ink is dry. The deal is done. After today, I'll never have to face Nora again, but I want her to walk away knowing I'm not scared of her. That I'll never be scared of her. She has no control over me, and now, she has no control over Brittni and Makya either. The ironclad contract we just signed ensures that.

I can't wait to be done with all this so I can take them to their new permanent home.

Home.

I know from experience how much a difference having an actual home can make. The day I found mine in Coty changed my life forever.

Tears gather in my eyes, but I blink them back just as fast.

"So what will you tell *my* daughters?" Nora sneers, pulling out her pack of cigarettes while we're still inside the building.

"I'll tell them while most people only have one mom, they had two...just during different periods. One for their first several years, and one for the rest of their lives." My voice cracks on the last part and I have to stop and collect myself.

I'm not naïve enough to think that explanation will suffice. The terms of the independent adoption made today will keep me from being able to divulge everything, but I wouldn't want to anyway. Some things are better left unsaid.

"What will *you* tell them?"

Nora screws her lip up at me. "When?"

"When you say goodbye?"

"Simple." With a shrug, she fits a cigarette to her already puckered mouth, mumbling around it, "Nothing."

Her daughters? Please. That's how much she considers those girls hers, she didn't even plan on saying a final goodbye to them.

Unable to hold myself back another second, I surge forward and rip the cigarette from her lips, gripping her shoulders in both hands.

"Angela, as your attorney, I have to advise you—"

I ignore Marshall's warning. I ignore his hand on my elbow. I ignore the voice in the back of my head saying not to give this woman anything else, least of all credit. But…it's not about me. None of this is.

Past the lump in my throat, I look Nora in the eyes and tell her, "Thank you. You played an important role in our lives. You were *my* daughters' first mother. If it wasn't for you, I wouldn't have them. Just as I'm thanking you now, they should get to tell you goodbye."

She rolls her eyes and blows out a loud sigh, the kind that indicates hard work. She doesn't know the first thing about hard work. She won't even have to lift a finger for the next few years. Longer, if she spends wisely.

Nora brings her gaze back to mine, a cruel smirk playing on her now empty lips. "And if I say I don't want to?"

I shake her shoulders once before letting her go. Marshall's hand falls away a second later.

"Don't. Don't say it. Keep it to yourself. For once in your fucking life, Nora, think of Brittni and Makya, and give them this one last thing. Let them get some kind of closure."

They deserve more than that, but that's on me to give them now, not Nora. I'll give them the reassurance all orphans seek out, the kind I searched for myself. They will probably always have at least one "what-if" floating around their heads, and while I can't silence them all, I can try to silence this one today. I'll even hold their hands through it. I took the day off from work to spend on this, on them...to spend *with* them.

"I have to use the toilet." Nora sneers in my direction, then Marshall's.

On her way to the bathroom, she pulls out another cigarette, her lighter already tucked between her thumb and palm.

I wait until the door closes behind her to let my shoulders droop completely. I want to hate her so bad, but I can't. Not wholly. I have to love at least some part of her, the part that made my girls, because that'll always be there.

"She knows it's illegal to smoke indoors in Washington, right?"

"She knows," I tell Marshall. "She just doesn't give a shit."

"I hope she doesn't set off the smoke detectors." He runs a hand through his graying hair, reminding me of his son when he's nervous. "I think it'd be best for everybody if you went ahead without her. You know, go get the girls by yourself."

His statement lingers in the air until I send it away with a headshake. It'd be easier for Nora, and it'd be easier for me, but it wouldn't be easier for Brittni and Makya. Not in the long run. I need them to understand that they were not given up, they were chosen by somebody else—somebody who wanted them infinitely more.

"Not for everybody." I turn for the entrance. "I'll wait for her outside."

They're getting their goodbye.

My first step outside my eyes shut against the overhead sunshine. A crisp draft blows past, tickling my lashes on my cheeks, and I lift my chin in the air, inhaling the distinctly autumn scents of bonfires and hay bales and falling leaves.

The sound of screeching tires has me cracking my eyes open sooner than I was hoping.

Bentlee?

Bentlee parks her lifted Toyota Tundra in the middle of the small parking lot, then she opens the driver's door. Hopping out, she comes around the tall front end, wearing a pair of tight jeans and hoodie with a vest over it. She's also holding a grocery bag of some sort. Whatever's in it, isn't big. It might even be empty.

"I can't believe we beat them," she says.

"Umm."

Behind Bentlee's truck, Paige's Suburban flies into the lot, too. She's out and meeting us in front of their vehicles before I can even register what's happening.

Bentlee smiles triumphantly over at her, bragging, "We beat the boys."

"Of course we did." Paige snorts, joking, "They're getting lazy in their old age."

"Hey! I'm older than all of you."

"Cougar." Paige winks at Bentlee, making her blush. For pants, she's still in scrubs, but has a tee on that says *Wife. Mom. Biker.* Did she leave from work?

"What are you two doing here?"

"You know how you asked me to take Coty and Jace home from the Fall Fest?"

I nod. I didn't give Paige a reason and she didn't ask for one. We all keep spare car seats and boosters in our vehicles in case something comes up. And like I told Coty, something did.

Bentlee says, "Rebel told me why. You ran into the girls?"

"Yeah, they were there that night. That doesn't explain how you found me here though."

Bentlee points at Paige, who grimaces as she says, "Ty."

My shoulders bunch near my ears all over again.

"Tysen knows I'm here?"

"My brother knows you left the shop this morning with no timeline for returning. It was a dead giveaway."

"Not really. I could've been going anywhere."

"But you didn't. We checked." She motions between herself and Bentlee. "We looked up your location and saw exactly where you went—my father-in-law's. We figured it was only a matter of time before you went back for those girls and we weren't about to miss it."

Bentlee lifts the bag in her hold. "I even bought lice treatment. Just in case."

I'm not surprised Rebel told her bonus mom about the Fall Fest. I didn't tell her not to. And I guess I shouldn't be surprised Bentlee and Paige figured out what I was doing on their own. We agreed to share our locations with each other years ago, when we all started taking turns carpooling each other's kids around. But I didn't expect…this—their unwavering support without fully knowing what I was up to.

"That is what you're doing, right? Getting Brit and Kya back?"

"Yeah. We just finished." I glance back at the building,

wondering how much longer Nora's planning on dragging this out. The sooner I can get the girls out of that house and into mine, the sooner I can tell Coty everything. Now that the wives know, it's only a matter of time before their husbands do too, and I want to be the one to break the news to Coty.

We have a lot to discuss.

Paige shrugs. "We always show up for each other when our family grows."

"And we know you'd never ask us to, which is why we did it on our own." Bentlee takes a deep breath and gestures behind me. "I remember how hard this was for me when I went through it with Shawn. Mediation with him felt like selling my soul to the lowest, least-deserving bidder. And from everything you told us about Nora, well, we just wanted to be here for you."

"You were there for me when the twins were born. Left straight from work the day my water broke, then didn't leave my side for three weeks after I gave birth. I couldn't have done it without you." Paige's eyes grow watery, and I feel my own start to blur, too.

"Yes, you could've."

"You took Hunter for us when I went into labor with Blaze. You even brought him to the hospital at three o'clock in the morning just so he could be the first to meet his sister. Of course we'd be here to help you."

"Thank you," I whisper through the tears streaming down my lips.

All three of us chuckle as we wipe at our own faces.

"I thought you had Jace today," I say to Bentlee. Coty was supposed to drop him off to her before work.

"I do." She nods. "Or…I did. Karina's watching him right now."

"Oh, and I got us lunch," Paige says as she motions at her SUV. "That was before I knew the other two were coming though."

I look between my friends. "The other two?"

"I told you we beat them here. I caught sight of Marc in my rearview and floored it."

"Same. Beckett was trailing me up until a few miles back when I lost him." Paige laughs like this is a game.

Who am I kidding? To that couple, everything's a game.

"I didn't tell the boys."

"Then Coty must've. Where is he, by the way?"

I shake my head. "I didn't tell *any* of the boys."

They stop to consider each other, then me.

"They're on their way here."

The telltale sound of motorcycles, three to be exact, fills the air.

No, they're already here.

CHAPTER 8

Angela

Turning, we watch as one after another, Coty, Marc, and Beckett, file in on their crotch rockets, filling the rest of the parking lot with their loud machines and their even louder assessments sweeping over each of us.

"Angela, why do they think you're here?"

I wrack my brain before saying, "I don't even know *how* they knew I was here."

"Probably the GPS Beckett snuck on everybody's phones."

Bentlee and I both gape at Paige, making her laugh again. I didn't approve sharing my location with Beckett, only Bentlee and Paige. How the hell did he manage that?

Removing his black helmet, Coty dismounts his bike first, immediately setting his accusatory glare on me.

Ty could've just as easily told Coty the same thing he told Paige, and I have no doubt if Beckett knew where I was, he'd offer the information up to his best friend without hesitation. Marc would get involved, because when isn't he? But, if that's true, why do they seem…mad?

"Girl, what did you do?"

The three of us look from one to the other, each pair of eyes more anxious than the last.

"What I had to."

"I know that feeling."

"We all do," Paige agrees with Bentlee. "It's been ingrained in our chemical makeup since the moment we became mothers." Facing the men now stalking toward us, she steps in front of me and sighs. "This is gonna suck."

"What is?"

Bentlee's the one who answers me as she positions herself shoulder to shoulder with Paige. "Going against our husbands."

"I can handle them myself."

"We know you can, but you shouldn't have to all the time," Bentlee says without taking her eyes off the approaching men. "You stand up for everybody else, including us, despite the odds. Let us stand up for you for once."

The backs of their heads distort in front of me and I try to wipe at my eyes again as inconspicuously as I can.

Once the men have shortened the distance between their trio and ours, Paige calls out, "That's far enough, boys!"

Beckett's steps falter. "You gotta be fuckin' kidding me."

"Not at all, baby. I need you to stay where you are."

"Why?"

Bentlee answers him though, explaining, "Because my husband's wearing his worst scowl, the one he uses when heads are about to roll, and we don't want anybody losing their head today, especially not one of ours."

Between the girls' shoulders, I catch a peek of Marc's murderous expression. Which isn't all that uncommon for him to have, but him aiming it at me is.

"What are you doing, Bentlee?" her glowering husband asks.

"Same thing you're doing I imagine."

"You're sticking up for *her*?"

The way he says "her" twists my insides because while it's obvious he means me, his reason isn't.

"You know how it goes." His wife sticks her hands in her pockets and rocks back on her heels. "Family first."

"Always," Paige finishes.

Hands out wide, Beckett bursts, "We're fucking family, dream!"

"So is Angela."

"What about Jace? He's not family?" Coty's voice is nothing but pain and anger.

At the mention of our son's name, I push through the wall of protection my friends are graciously trying to offer me and stand on my own—the way I've always been prepared to face my problems.

"Jace? What's wrong with Jace?"

"You tell me, Angela. Where is he?"

Coty told me before that I was his heaven, but the way he's looking at me now, it's like I'm his own personal hell.

I turn toward Bentlee, and brows furrowed, she rushes to tell him, "He should be with Karina."

Without waiting for his response, she pulls out her phone, and whatever she finds, she looks back up at me and shrugs.

"Nothing."

I check my phone, too. There's nothing from Karina, but there are several missed calls from Coty following one from the wedding planner. The wedding planner...

Did she call him and tell him what we discussed? Is that why he's so upset?

This is why I wanted to talk to him first.

"Karina?" I hear Coty repeat to himself. Louder, he asks, "So Jace isn't here?"

"No," Bentlee answers.

"Coty?" I tear my eyes from my screen to meet Coty's. "Why are you here?"

Taking slow, calculated steps, Coty comes right up to me, and seethes, "Why are you?" Only inches from my face, air pours through his nose on to mine.

"Coty," Paige warns, but I shake my head, letting her know it's okay. I appreciate the girls being cautious, but they know as well as I do Coty would never lay a hand on a woman. None of these men would.

We're all just passionate about the same thing—our family. To which my loyalty seems to be in question right now. Anything I've done is for this family though.

"I need to tell you something. It started at the Fall Fest—"

"Told you," Beckett scoffs.

Past Coty, I turn my stare on him, asking, "Told him what?"

"About you getting fucked in your back seat by some other guy."

Coty's words slap me across the face harder than either of his hands ever could, making me rear back at the same time a pair of gasps go off behind me.

"What are you talking about?"

"Don't even try it, Angie. I saw you."

"Saw me when?"

Coty answers for Beckett again, saying, "After the Fall Fest. On the security tapes at Pop One, he saw you cleaning the Jeep's back seat. When you fucking ditched me and our son to go—"

Cutting him off, I say, "Don't finish that sentence," my voice sharp as nails and just as unforgiving. I already let him get away with saying the baseless accusation aloud once, I won't make that mistake again.

Amid the tense silence, Bentlee asks, "That's the evidence you guys are going off of?"

Paige cracks up laughing. "What kind of freaky sex are you having that requires a full interior detail afterward?"

"Ask Coty." I meet my fiancé's hardened gaze with my own. "He's the only person I've ever had sex with in my Jeep, except we never make it to the back seat, do we?" I ask him with a head tilt before admitting, "I usually just mount him in the front seat."

The corner of Coty's lips quirk before he can stop it.

"Dayum, neighbor girl, we didn't need to know all that."

"You're the one making assumptions about my sex life, Beckett."

"Pull your heads out of your asses, boys!" Paige shouts, then claps like she's a teacher getting her class of misfits' attention. "Angela would never cheat on Coty."

"I didn't say she did!" Marc shouts back before waving at our tallest friend. "It was him."

"I didn't say she did, *per se*," Beckett explains with the kind of innocence a bank robber has when he gets caught holding the duffle bag full of cash. "It's just… Angie, shit looked bad."

"You could've asked. You should've. And I would've answered you honestly."

Below drawn eyebrows, Coty's chocolate eyes appear even darker as they search mine.

"Would you have?"

Yes.

Probably.

Maybe.

I don't know. This all happened so fast. I didn't have time to play out every hypothetical. Aside from the few I told him when we were first getting to know each other, I haven't lied to Coty, but this was an extreme situation, one I acted on out of pure instinct. Those moms that lift cars off their children, they don't stop to question if it'll ruin their back, they just fucking lift. I lifted and now my back's out.

"I don't know," I confess.

"Will you now?"

"Yes."

"What were you cleaning off your back seat?"

"Lice."

"Pube lice?" Beckett guesses incorrectly.

"Do you mean crabs?" Marc asks with one of his less-hostile scowls.

"Same thing."

"It's like their minds are programmed to always go straight to sex," Bentlee murmurs, and I nod.

"Especially that one."

No doubt about it, Beckett Meyers is a thirty-one-year-old teenager.

"Heads up, big guy!" Bentlee yells a second before a small box goes sailing through the air in a high arc over our heads.

Beckett catches it, mumbling, "The fuck?"

"Head lice," I say with a roll of my eyes, before repeating what Paige just said, "I would *never* cheat on Coty."

"Told you," Paige mocks, earning a groan from her husband.

"Then can someone please explain what the fuck she is doing here?" Marc asks. "And why you two are here?"

"We came to celebrate," his wife answers simply.

"With a lice removal kit? Some fucking party." Beckett flings the box, sending it sideways before it falls to the asphalt between him and Marc with a *clatter*.

"Your husband's such a baby sometimes," I tell Paige since I'm just about done with him.

As if to further prove my point, Beckett crosses his thick arms over his chest to literally pout.

Yep, I'm done.

Paige chuckles while sauntering up to her husband. "He's *always* a baby."

As soon as she's in reach, he shoots out those tree branches he calls arms and hugs her, making her laugh even harder.

Bentlee goes over and picks the kit up, saying, "If anything's broken inside, you owe me twenty-five dollars."

"I'll pay it, mama," Marc tells her, grabbing one of his wife's back pockets to drag her to him. "We all fucked this one up."

"What exactly did we fuck up? What are you celebrating?" Coty asks.

Paige and Bentlee remain quiet, giving me the floor.

I take a deep breath, not stopping until my lungs ache. I can't believe I get to actually say this.

"I adopted Brittni and Makya."

Relief trickles in to replace the anger in Coty's every muscle. It's slow but it's spreading. "What? How?"

"Independent adoption. Marshall got the ball rolling yesterday and today we finalized everything. We just got done."

"Fuck," he breathes out, turning around and dragging a hand down his face. Almost immediately, he returns to me, grasping my jaw in his hands and pressing his forehead to mine. "I'm sorry. I'm so sorry. I thought—"

"You thought the worst of me. You thought I was fu—"

"Don't finish that sentence." Coty slams his eyes shut on a wince. "Please."

"How could you even think that? After everything we've been through together... And Jace? What does he have to do with any of this?"

When Coty opens his eyes again, they're on the move, roaming every inch of my face.

"We saw you were at Marshall's and we..."

"Not we. You two," Marc says.

"It was mostly Marc."

Beckett earns himself a colorful curse from Marc.

"I, okay? *I* thought you were trying to take Jace from me."

"Oh my God, Coty. Take Jace? What gave you that idea?"

"The call I got from the wedding planner where she said you were considering cancelling the wedding. It sounded like you were running."

"I'm not running. I was never going anywhere."

"Then why did you tell her that?"

"I was only asking about our options in the event I'm unable to cover my portion anymore."

"Can you cover it?"

I shake my head.

"Why? What'd you have to give up?"

My gaze falls to my hands gripping my phone, and I whisper, "Everything." I'm officially broke. Broker than broke. All of my accounts, checking, savings, everything, it's all been wiped.

The front door to Marshall's firm opens, and I blink long and hard before turning my head over my shoulder to watch Nora strut outside and over to her light-blue Tercel.

Her hand on the driver's side handle, she takes in the

scene, and asks with way too much enthusiasm, "Should we reschedule?"

"No. I'll follow you there now," I tell her.

"Wow," Coty mocks. "Looks like you proved your mom right."

Switching my attention back to Coty, I find him wearing the same expression he had when he arrived—eyes narrowed, jaw clenching, elbows bowed.

"How so?"

"You did exactly what she said you'd do. You chose yourself."

When did she tell him that?

I straighten, solidifying my spine. "I chose everyone but myself. I chose the girls, and even though you're too upset to see it right now, I chose you, too."

There's no way Coty would've approved of us doing anything to jeopardize the wedding, not so close to it, and I needed my money—every dollar—to give Nora. I would've handed over anything to get the girls out of her care, which she knew and so she went for it, *all* of it. Coty has to understand that. If this was any other time, without a wedding on the line, he would've been sitting next to me in that conference room today. He would've been writing a similar check but from his own account because Coty's generosity knows no bounds. He'd give someone the shirt off his back. He'd give up anything to help someone else…except me.

That's why I didn't put him in the position to even consider it.

"How did you choose me?"

"Because I knew. I knew what it would come down to and I knew you wouldn't be able to decide."

"Decide between what? Getting the girls back or getting married? Were those the choices?"

"Not exactly. We can still—"

"No, we can't." He gestures to my hands. "You didn't choose me then, and you didn't choose me now."

I glance down, seeing what he sees—my bare hands—then rush forward, saying, "I couldn't—"

He backs away, his own hands up like he doesn't want me near him. "The wedding is off."

"Coty. It's—"

Nora's honking prevents me from saying anything more.

Beckett and Marc both throw her dirty looks, muttering under their breath as they start to roll their bikes out of her way.

As soon as her path's clear, she's leaving, and I don't trust her to wait for me. God knows what would happen if I let her out of my sight.

Shit. I have to go.

"I'm sorry," I mouth to Coty before sprinting over to my Jeep and getting in. Gripping the steering wheel as tight as I can, I shake my upper half, gritting my teeth to keep the scream in. He called it off. *He* called it off. Coty doesn't want to marry me anymore. Does he want to be with me at all?

A panic so chaotic and consuming claws its way up my ribs, into my throat, then bursts from my mouth on a hysterical sob.

I don't even bother backing up and going through the parking lot. I just shift into Drive, then gun it up and over the parking block, through the landscaping, across the sidewalk, and on to the open road.

Coty's words follow me the entire way to Nora's. *"You didn't choose me then, and you didn't choose me now."*

Round and round I go, back to the beginning we know. Last time I took on all the risk in order to save those I love it didn't work out the way I planned either. But last time, Coty chose me back.

This time, he didn't.

CHAPTER 9

Angela

"**M**OMMY BIRTHDAY?"
I gasp into the phone, then ask Jace,
"Who told you?"
"Daddy."

Coty mumbles something and just the sound of his voice makes my heart ache. I want to hear that voice in person again, not just over the phone as background noise. I miss him talking directly to me, but he's only willing to speak to me through our three-year-old right now.

Coty hasn't been home since the showdown. He suggested—via text—that he'd keep Jace out of the house for me while I treated the girls for lice. It's been three days since I've seen him, hugged him, kissed him.

Coty and I have never spent a night away from each other. Never. Not since we moved in together out here in the house he built specifically for us to grow a family in, to grow together in. Once he branched out from Pop The Hood, he still made it a habit to call or text me at least once during the day, just to check in or say hi. Some people would find that suffocating, but not me. I know it's because he genuinely means it.

Meant it?

Not being on speaking terms means we haven't discussed what happens next. Or what happens now, for that matter. Our wedding got cancelled but does that mean we're over? Like *over* over? Because I'm not over anything, least of all

Coty. I could never be over Coty. The longing I felt for him the moment I left him standing in front of Marshall's office has doubled each day I've gone without seeing him, and three days later, I'm practically choking on my yearning. I need Coty like the moon needs the sun. Without him, I have no shine. Without him, everything's just dark.

I sigh, telling Jace, "Yeah, it's Mommy's birthday."

As far as birthdays go, this one might be the worst, and I've had some bad birthdays in my lifetime. I'm not only missing Coty and our son, I'm also missing the rest of the family.

I glance around the house. The girls and I have been cooped up inside for three days now, we could use some new scenery. I spent the morning combing what felt like every strand of hair on both Brittni's and Makya's heads—twice— so I know they're bug-free.

I cover the phone to ask, "What do you girls say to getting out of here?"

Makya nods enthusiastically.

"Brit?"

Brittni shrugs her shoulders, a little more reluctant than her younger sister. "I guess."

Even though they could technically go back to school starting Monday, I probably won't send them for at least another week. Not only to be sure the lice is gone, but to let their eyelashes grow in a little because middle schoolers can be brutal. It's a good thing Brittni's cousin is the toughest girl in school.

Harley, Terra, and Tysen's son, Diesel, will be happy to welcome Makya back to their elementary school. Our family is tightknit like that. No matter how much time passes, or what happens, we don't give up on each other.

We don't give up on each other.

Our relationship is not just between two people who love each other. It never was. The life Coty and I share together has been intricately woven by not only our own hands, but also the hands around us—the stitching unable to come undone as easily as other relationships. Other *simple* relationships, because with us, it's not so simple.

Neither is this. This is difficult.

Or maybe it's not; I just made it so. It's the only way I know though. The easy route's never appealed to me, even in times of desperation, mainly because I don't trust it. Things that are easy to get are easy to lose.

The money I lost adopting the girls didn't feel like losing at all because what I gained means more to me than money ever could. I've never considered money to be a permanent fixture in my life. I valued it but it wasn't *valuable* to me because I've lived without it and survived. Losing Coty, however, that feels like the biggest loss of all.

Coty wasn't just a part of my life, he was my life. He *is* my life.

"Are you at Funcle Beckett's house or Uncle Marc's?" I ask Jace.

"Bett-ett's house."

My heartrate spikes at the idea of seeing both Jace and Coty.

"Can I come see you?"

"Uh-huh. Come see me at Bett-ett's."

Coty murmurs something I'm almost positive I won't like.

"I'll be fast," I say, in case Coty's close enough to hear me. I'll pull the birthday card if I have to. I just want to see them.

"Mommy fast."

Coty's deep voice clearly rumbles, "No, she's not. Daddy's fast."

Jace giggles, repeating, "Mommy fast."

A grin pulls at my lips. He's saying it just to get under his dad's skin now. Fine by me. Whatever gets Coty to loosen up a bit, maybe even talk to me directly.

I didn't do any of the things he accused me of. I didn't even consider doing the things he accused me of. I didn't cheat on him. I didn't run. I didn't try taking Jace from him. I didn't cancel the wedding. And I sure as hell didn't sell my engagement ring.

That's not to say I'm completely innocent. I did break his trust. I did lie to him. And I did hide things from him. But I thought…I mean, I *hoped*…that Coty would do what he always does. I hoped he'd read me and read my heart, and see that I really did what I thought I had to. He knows as well as I do that once siblings are put into the system, they can be separated—easily. Not all foster families can, or will, take on more than one child at a time; so every single day siblings that enter foster care together are split up. And that's assuming the girls even made it into the system. Nora was keeping them home from school, not for the same reasons I am, but so nobody would see how bad off Brittni and Makya were and report her again.

Any person in our family would've done the same. They would've.

They could've…if I let them.

Now that I'm not facing that same fight-or-flight reaction I've always struggled with, I can look back and admit I panicked. I could've stopped to talk to someone, anyone, about what was going on. Paige and Bentlee were right. I'm used to taking on battles singlehandedly. It doesn't matter that it wasn't me I was fighting for, I still pushed Coty away to win, and that's not the kind of victory I want on my record. He's been in my corner for so long, he's had my back in every situation. The only fight I haven't encountered is the one *for* Coty.

"Actually, Jace, I think Mommy's faster," I say, then hold my breath. Will he repeat it?

"Mommy faster?"

A chuckle leaves my lips. "Yep, I'm faster. Way faster."

"Mommy faster."

There's some rustling on the other end before one of the best sounds I've heard in three days comes across the speaker as Coty says, "I'm faster."

I hang up wearing a full-blown smile. He spoke to me. Maybe he's open to listening to me, too.

Jogging up the stairs, I tell the girls to get their shoes on and meet me in the Jeep.

I chose Coty then, and I'm choosing him now.

CHAPTER 10

Coty

THE LONG GRASS BRUSHES AGAINST THE LEGS OF my jeans as I look out over the canyon. My property sits below Beck's off to the side, and Marc's is far enough away in the distance that I can barely make out someone's cloud of dust behind them as they race around the track.

Angela's Jeep pulls from our garage and my shoulders sag watching her reverse down our driveway slowly.

Slowly, because I'm definitely the faster one of us.

Except for this week. I started out feeling behind on everything, and now, I am behind on everything.

Angela books it up Beck's driveway, but I don't move from my spot. I came out here as soon as she hung up. She can visit Jace. I'd never actually try to keep him from her, I just…I don't want to see her right now. I can't. If I see her without her engagement ring again, I'll fucking…I don't know.

I could rage at her, let out all the shit I've been keeping in since I first saw her finger missing the ring I proposed to her with, or I could fall at her feet and beg her to take me back because I miss her that. Fucking. Much. I *miss* Angela. I even miss the girls, too. I miss my entire family being together. I feel like I'm walking around with half my body missing. Every step I take is wobbly and unsure.

Which is why I'm so pissed off that she didn't trust me.

She did trust me, but only to choose her, not Brittni and

Makya. That's such bullshit. That's her own assumption. That's...

Fair.

It is. It's fair. My first—and usually only—thought has always been Angela. Without her...

I never wanted to be without her.

And now that I am, I remember why. This is fucking torture. I forgot what life before Angela was like—dull, hazy, pointless. Being with her is like living life in sharp focus, everything's so much clearer and makes more sense.

Nothing makes sense right now. Not what happened, not what I'm doing about it. I don't want to be away from her, but I don't know how to be around her either. I'm fucking livid.

We should be getting ready to exchange vows tomorrow.

But then we wouldn't have Brittni and Makya.

No, *she* wouldn't have Brittni and Makya.

Does it really matter? As long as they're out of that house of horrors, that's what really matters. I would've chosen those girls over anything, just...why'd it have to be our wedding?

Fuck. Angela's right. I would've flinched, and that flinch could've cost Brit and her sister. I would've struggled to make the right decision, but only in this specific circumstance. If our wedding wasn't in danger...

That's just it, our wedding wouldn't have been in danger if Angela came to me first. I would've found a way to get enough money to pay Nora off without draining Angela of everything. I'll always find a way around anything standing between Angela and the happiness I think she deserves.

Because that's where she's wrong. I wouldn't have chosen my own happiness of having Angela as my wife. I would've chosen *her* happiness. The girls being safe and sound would make her happy, happier than standing at an altar with a hundred and seventy-two faces staring at her.

Jesus. No wonder she didn't have any problem choosing between the girls and *that* wedding. She never wanted it. She said it herself, she only wanted our family and three kinds of cake.

If she hadn't sold her engagement ring, maybe I could've given her that kind of wedding. But that's the one decision I can't forgive her for making. I could forgive Angela anything, except that. That ring was a symbol of the love and hope and respect I've always had for her. I held on to it for *years*, waiting for the right time to give it to her. Her selling it, getting rid of it so quickly, so easily, is unforgivable. Angela doesn't put a lot of sentiment into material items, but for me, it was so much more than a piece of jewelry. Finally seeing that ring on her was like my past, present, and future coming together in one place.

Now it's just gone.

The Jeep stops at Beck's house and the girls get out, Makya first, then Brittni. God, I don't care what the papers say, those are my kids, too. Have been since I first laid eyes on them. Brittni and Makya were delivered to our front door with no shoes on their feet. They were sent to school, took the bus and everything, without shoes. No shoes, no socks. That wasn't an oversight. That was a fucking crime.

I wanted to say so fucking much to Nora when I saw her the other day. I wanted to tell her what a piece of shit she is and how those girls deserve better, but I didn't have to. My... Angela told her everything that needed to be said by getting the girls out of her clutches. I hate that she did it without me even knowing, but I'm glad she did it.

Angela gets out last and points at the house. Waiting until the girls disappear into the garage, she drapes her arm over her open door and stares at me with her head in her hand.

I thought she was here to see Jace. Is she planning on coming over here? I want her to as much as I don't.

I want her to.

But if I so much as open my mouth right now, I'm not even sure what'll come out.

I'm sorry.

I love you.

Fuck you.

Why?

It's all right on the tip of my tongue, so I grind my back molars together, gazing at the most frustratingly beautiful woman I've ever seen, held, kissed, made love to, bickered with, cursed at, grown alongside, parented with, and loved with every fucking bit of my mind, body, and soul.

Angela eventually shuts her door and starts the trek toward me. With each step she takes, I feel the weight that's been on my chest since Tuesday start to ease, allowing me to breathe fully for the first time in days.

Angela owns me wholly. It's never been more apparent than this moment. After spending the last three days without her, I'm in fucking ruins.

"Were you—"

"Just shut up," she says, still walking.

Jerking my head back, I frown as I shove my hands in my pockets.

"So, I'm the bad guy?"

A few feet away, she stops and just...stops. We stare at each other for a while, neither of us saying anything.

"Angela—"

"You always do this. You say the right thing. You do the right thing. You're the one that gets to smooth things over, but let me try this time, okay?"

I give her a nod, even though I don't always do the right thing. If I did, she'd be in my arms already. But I'll give her what she wants, what she needs. I've always given her that.

"When I saw the girls at the Fall Fest, they were…" She dabs her eyelids, pressing harder than she probably should. "They were…"

"Like they were when we first got them?" My voice is as cold as my veins feel envisioning Brittni and Makya on our doorstep last year. Bare feet, itchy, starving.

"Worse. So much worse. You have to understand, Coty, I was sick, fucking *sick* with worry about them."

Tears run down her cheeks despite her fingertips still attempting to dam the source, and I have to stop myself from going to her to wipe them off.

"I couldn't move on. I couldn't *breathe* without them."

That is a feeling I know all too well.

"You should've told me," I say after a hard swallow.

"I couldn't."

"Why?"

"You know why."

I clench my jaw. The wedding.

"I didn't care about the wedding."

She drops her hands to meet my eyes again. "That's not entirely true."

"No, it's not," I confess. I did care about that wedding. "But if you would've given me the chance, I would've found another way to marry you, Angela. I would've married you in our spare bathroom."

"You hate that bathroom."

"Exactly. I would've married you from our bed, in our rattiest pajamas, with an officiant on a video call. I would've married you *anywhere*." And that is true.

Her eyebrows lift over eyes that are normally clear and full of humor but are now red and full of…I can't tell. I used to be able to tell. I used to be really fucking good at telling exactly what she was feeling. How did I lose that so quickly?

"You're doing it again."

"What?"

"Stealing my thunder by giving a speech that's going to make me cry."

"You're already crying." I wave at her, my arm, hand, and fingers all reaching farther than I was planning until I almost brush her front. Once I touch her though, I don't think I'll be able to stop, and we need to have this talk. We need to have lots of talks. I never want to stop talking to her. Why the fuck did I think I'd be able to?

She wipes her face, saying, "You're not the bad guy, Coty. You could never be. You're the hero." All movement on her stops as she tells me, "You're *my* hero."

"You make it sound like I saved you," I say, glancing around like I didn't just hear the biggest compliment of my life.

"You did."

I look back at her, her seriousness almost too much.

"You're just trying to—"

"Marry you?" she finishes, but I don't answer. That's not what I was about to say. Is that what she's doing?

I study her, gauging.

Well, trying to gauge. She's…different right now. Or maybe I'm just seeing her differently now that I've been away from her for a few days. Living with someone, being around them every day, focused on them so closely, you don't notice all the changes they make like someone with a wider lens could. I've not only been looking at her, but also treating her, like the same girl I first met. But Angela's not her anymore. Gone is the girl from Creekwood and in her place is the woman from the canyon. She was always fierce but this is fucking staggering.

Angela drops to one knee, causing me to actually lurch forward.

"What are you doing?"

She pulls out a ring box and presents it to me without opening it.

"Angela?"

"I'm sorry I lied to you. I'm sorry I went behind your back. I'm sorry I risked and ultimately caused the cancellation of the big wedding I would've been miserable at."

"I knew it," I say, making both of us grin.

"I'm sorry I didn't tell you about Brittni and Makya sooner. I'm sorry I adopted them without your consent."

I just shrug. What can I say? I wish they were legally mine, but we've never needed papers to tell us who our family is.

Her eyebrows crinkle, but she pushes on, saying, "I'm sorry I'm as broke now as I was when we first met."

I scoff. "I never gave a shit about that."

"I'm sorry I made you question my loyalty to you, to our family."

Humiliation sweeps through me, trying to shield my eyes from the harsh truth of my absolute dumbfuckery. I accused Angela of cheating on me with the weakest, most non-existent evidence ever. The women were right to laugh at us when we came at them with that shit. We were so goddamn stupid.

I was so goddamn stupid. To consider it, was stupid. To actually say it, was so much worse. The second the accusation left my mouth, it also left a burn mark on my heart because I know it did on Angela's, too.

I make sure I don't blink as I pin her with the most sincerity I'm fucking capable of to say, "You didn't make me do anything. My own insecurities made me question myself and my beliefs because I *know* you wouldn't cheat on me, just like I knew you wouldn't actually try to take Jace from me either. No one's more sorry than I am for not only saying those things, but even thinking them. I'm so fucking sorry. You are—"

"Coty?"

"Yeah, babe?"

"This is my speech."

Our mouths mirror each other's as they both spread.

"Sorry. It's just the way everything unfolded that day, I didn't know what to think. I was so…"

"Scared?"

"Fucking terrified," I admit for what might be the first time in my life. Being scared is foreign to me. Handling fear effectively, even more so. "It changed me until I didn't even recognize myself. I got—"

"Reckless?"

Reckless. That's a good way to describe how I felt that day thinking I was on the verge of losing the people I love most. I was downright irrational.

That must've been how Angela felt seeing the girls in danger. Damn.

"Yeah. I got reckless." My gaze drops to her hands holding the ring box out to me. "Just like you."

"I was reckless…but not exactly careless." She opens the box, revealing what's inside.

I look from it to her, tears making it hard to see but not impossible. That's definitely the engagement ring I gave her last week.

"I chose you. You're the one that taught me the definition of unconditional love, both giving and receiving it. Your heartbeat is the best music I've fallen asleep to, and the only sound I crave waking up to. Your eyes…" She pauses, swallowing. "Your eyes are the sweetest treat I've ever been addicted to. I fell for them before I even saw them. Even behind a visor, I could *feel* you looking at me. It's the same feeling I get now, ten years later. No amount of time will ever change that because ours is the first happily ever after I've ever believed in. I *choose* you, Coty."

Goddamn, what a speech.

But I have to know.

"How did you…"

"I never sold it. I wouldn't. I just didn't wear it to the mediation because I didn't want Nora to see it and get any ideas. It's my ring and will forever be my ring, just like you'll forever be my husband."

"Husband?"

"We can use whatever term you want, as long as you're mine," she says through a slight grimace, quoting me from a long, long time ago.

"I'm yours. You know I'm yours. Have been since I laid eyes on you," I repeat back to her, somehow meaning it more now than I did back then, and I fucking *meant* it then. "You also know what term I want to use, but only if you're ready."

"*If* I'm ready?" She arches an eyebrow. "Coty Walsh, will you make me the happiest woman to ever walk this planet by marrying me and becoming my husband?"

"Yes. Hell yes." I drop to both knees in front of her, taking her face in my hands. "When are we talking?"

She smiles, saying, "Now."

"Now?"

"Are you busy?"

I laugh. "Nothing could keep me from marrying you today."

"You don't mind sharing an anniversary with my birthday?"

"I don't mind sharing anything with you."

Doubt clouds her eyes as they narrow.

"I have nothing to offer you in return."

"Money comes and it goes, but love, our love, that's forever. All I need is you." I pull her to me, but just before kissing her, I add, "And maybe a ring because you just proposed to me with yours."

Her lips spread against mine.

"I can't afford one."

"We can. Everything that's mine is yours, including my money. No more separate accounts, no more separate anything. I want to share everything with you."

Angela's hands cover mine, and she says, "Let's start with your last name," then kisses me using more conviction than a speech ever could.

CHAPTER 11

Angela

"OKAY, THE CHRISTENSEN CREW SHOULD BE here any minute. And Beckett and Marc are on their way over now," Paige tells me from the front seat, her long legs stretched out of the open door, on to the ground.

"Beckett? I thought he was officiating?" The last few hours have passed in a blur of activity to pull this wedding off, one of which Beckett was supposed to be using to get ordained online.

"Then who would give you away?" Beckett asks, coming up beside my Jeep as Bentlee teases my hair in the back seat.

Beside him, Marc asks seriously, "Me?"

"Pssh. No. Not without me."

"So who's officiating?"

They step aside, gesturing to the man who used to be my stepbrother, his auburn hair styled to perfection and his usual preppy outfit finally fitting the occasion.

"Drew," I say, smiling so big my cheeks hurt. He made it. He's just as busy as the rest of us now with his own family.

"You look beautiful, Angela," he tells me, giving my cheek a kiss before stepping back.

"Yeah, Angie. Our boy's gonna cream his pants when he sees you."

"Romantic," Bentlee mutters behind me.

Marc shoves Beckett while I look down at the dress I

bought right off the floor an hour and a half ago, using Coty's money, which he insists is now mine. The triangle-cut top is made up of black lace with a very, very low back, and the floor-length tulle skirt is ombre black and mulberry. It is anything but traditional, just like us.

This is more our style than a big wedding at a big venue with a big audience. We're getting married on a hillside overlooking where our home is, where our family is, surrounded by the people that matter most to us. We're doing it the way we live our life, on our own time, and at our own speed.

"Who's watching the kids?"

"Coty," Paige says, making the guys chuckle mischievously.

"Marc, you know how that ended for you at our wedding," Bentlee scolds her husband.

"Don't worry, the Christensen men will pitch in as soon as they get here. Karina's already over there helping him out right now." Fake coughing, he adds, "Hunter and Rebel, too."

Everybody, including Drew, goes quiet.

"Those two are actually together and not fighting?" I ask, peeking up at Marc from under my long, mascara-coated lashes.

"They don't fight each other," Bentlee says. "Just…" Her hands pause in my hair.

"Each other's crushes," Paige offers.

Marc shakes his head. "Hunter doesn't fight anybody."

"Double standard," Beckett gripes, causing all three of us women to groan and cuss him out at once. He has no room to talk.

I don't know what the deal with Rebel and Hunter is—I don't think any of us do really—but I hope they get it figured out because they can't keep going down this path. Rebel could end up in juvie before she even makes it to high school, and Hunter will probably die a virgin because Rebel refuses to let any other girls near him. She's like a human force field that zaps anyone that gets too close to her stepbrother who's not technically her stepbrother.

"What if it's because they're…"

"They're fourteen and fifteen," Marc says quickly. "They're not doing anything."

"You wanna know what I was doing at fourteen and fifteen?"

Every single one of us replies, "No," to Beckett, effectively shutting him up…if only for a moment.

"Hunter's a good boy," Paige says, pushing to standing. Wearing a leather jacket over her striped maxi-dress, she gives her book-page flowers an impressed look, and murmurs, "Who knew all that napkin rolling would've paid off?"

I told her about seeing the literary blooms at another ceremony and she offered to recreate them for me. She did a great job. They look exactly like the ones I remember.

"And Rebel's a good girl," I agree, taking the "flower" bouquet from her. "Together, they're…"

"My kids," Marc growls. "Can we drop this? Isn't there a wedding or something we're supposed to be doing?"

Bentlee finishes separating my curls to perfection, so I slide out slowly, making sure I don't snag my dress's somewhat poufy skirt on anything. She follows me out, her husband helping keep her turtleneck sweater dress from riding up.

After I thank both women for everything, they trudge over to where I'll be meeting and marrying Coty somewhere on the other side of my Jeep. I've been careful to only look forward and not behind me, something I should do more of.

Drew eventually leaves to get in position, then it's just me and two of my old neighbors.

"Well? Can you believe we finally made it here?" I ask them both, and they smile, shaking their heads.

None of us could've guessed this is where we'd be, or how long it'd take us, but I'm glad we managed to stay together. Beckett and Marc are as much my safe place as Coty.

"I thought it'd be sooner," Marc admits.

"I thought you'd make our boy wait forever. Poor bastard's been pining after you for a decade."

They both have wives and kids now, but they've always been these amazingly complicated men that would take on the world for those they love, whether they were asked to or not. I've had the pleasure of watching Beckett and Marc grow these last ten years, and while there have definitely been some growing pains along the way, I've enjoyed every minute of it.

Except for when they accused me of cheating on Coty. I didn't enjoy that.

"Thanks for keeping Coty company while he waited. And thanks for not giving up on me…fully."

"We didn't give up on you. We just…"

"I know. As much as it hurt to have you two turn against me, even momentarily," I add at Marc's clenched jaw because he can say it was Beckett all he wants, but he was there, too, confronting me with his scariest scowl. "I understand you were just trying to protect your friend, your brother. I'd expect nothing less."

"We're sorry we doubted you."

"Will you forgive us?" Beckett gives his best puppy-dog eyes.

I wait a minute, letting them sweat a bit before rolling

my eyes and saying, "Of course. I love you too much to stay mad at you." Besides, I have a pretty good idea how they can make it up to me.

"Do not!" Beckett shouts, pinching the bridge of his nose. "Do not make me cry right now."

"I'm sorry, too," I tell them honestly. "I'm sorry I didn't tell either of you what I was planning." Beckett hates being in the dark about anything because he doesn't like being left out, period, and Marc's kept enough of his own secrets to know it doesn't always end well. It did for us this time, but only because our family is strong enough to survive anything now. Each of us has our own individual strengths, but together, we're impenetrable.

I'll never lose sight of that again.

"We would've had your back."

I nod as I glance from Marc to Beckett.

"We would've got those girls for you, Angie."

"I know you would've, but I needed to prove I could do it myself. They're more…mine that way."

They glance at each other over my head, and Marc shakes his, saying, "Still."

"Still what?"

Beckett answers, saying, "You still question your worth."

"You're worthy of Brittni and Makya, Angela," Marc tells me.

Just as serious, Beckett says, "You're worthy of this family."

"You're worthy of me," Coty says unexpectedly.

We look over to see him standing several feet away, dressed in an all-black suit only broken up by his crisp white dress shirt peeking out between the jacket's lapels, taking in each of his best friends before settling his gaze on me, starting at my feet and making his way up to my face. Shimmery pools fill his eyes and he doesn't so much as blink, adamant that I see it all.

That same wedding I stumbled across with the literary blooms, I remember the groom and bride shared a similar first moment. It was almost palpable—the pure adoration on her part and the complete reverence on his. I was so jealous, jealous of the look he gave her, of the deep love they so obviously shared, because I never thought I'd have it. Now I just feel sorry for that couple. Their connection doesn't come close to ours.

"You're worthy," he says, his glassy mocha-swirl eyes holding mine.

"And you're early," Beckett tells him. "We're supposed to give her to you."

"She's not yours to give. She's mine to take."

"Actually, fuckwad, she is. I claimed her for us from the start. Remember, Angie?"

I shake my head, my loose curls tickling my back from the movement.

"Yeah, it was back at Creekwood, that one night you fell asleep on the couch while we were watching *Tremors*. I asked if we could keep you."

"Did I answer you?"

Beckett grins at Marc, then Coty.

It's Marc who says, "You didn't really have to."

"I think this is answer enough." Beckett holds his hands out, gesturing to the canyon.

"Isn't it bad luck to see the bride before she even makes it to the aisle?" I ask instead. Of course they can keep me. Theirs is the only family I've ever felt like I truly belonged.

"Uh, neighbor girl, there is no aisle. We're having a wedding in a fucking meadow on three hours' notice."

I roll my eyes. "You know what I mean."

"I wanted to keep an eye on you," Coty says more like a threat than anything—a delicious threat—and even though it's a chilly day and I'm not wearing much, my groom's words are what have me fighting a shiver as we stare each other down.

"I'm not running," I promise softly but vehemently.

"Sorry. I misspoke." With one hand in his suit pocket, he closes the distance, putting us toe to toe. "I'm going to keep an eye on you. Today and every day after. Not because I think you'll run, but because if you do, I want to be right next to you."

"Sucker," Beckett breathes on a laugh, and Coty puts his erect middle finger in his face, not taking his eyes off mine.

"That might be difficult."

The space between Coty's eyebrows crinkles. "Why?"

"Because I'm faster."

His face smooths out on a smile very similar to the one I feel myself wearing.

The song I chose as our opener starts up from the area we should be congregating right now. It's "Collide" by Rachel Platten, and after listening to the first forty-five seconds, Coty whispers, "This is for me?"

"This is for you."

His forehead kisses mine and our bodies start swaying together, slow and steady, the familiar tang of his spicy coconut scent infusing the fresh air around us.

"I can't promise you perfect 'cause I'm not perfect," he tells me.

Recognizing the same vows he told me a decade ago when we first made our relationship official, I say, "I can't promise you easy 'cause it won't be."

"But I can promise to be here for you through it all no matter what, loving you in any way you'll allow me for as long as I'm breathing."

"Whether that makes you my husband or not is up to you—"

"I'm your husband."

I laugh before finishing, "But my feelings remain the same."

"I see your wreckage and want to fix my own just so I can be the armor yours is missing."

He's upheld every word, every day.

"I love you, Coty."

"I love you, Angela." With his palms grazing my bare back, his fingertips tickle the skin along my backbone. Eyes darkening, he whispers, "You look fucking gorgeous."

"You're just trying to—"

"Marry you? Damn right I am."

"Jesus fuck, now I understand why you two aren't married yet. You can't get out of each other's faces long enough to walk down the fucking aisle."

"There is no aisle," I remind Beckett with a smug grin.

Coty growls, "Fuck you," at his friend, the spell now broken.

"See? I'm telling you, murder's the vibe."

I have to pull back from Coty to ask, "What?" *Murder?*

Ignoring me, Marc pulls the "flowers" from my hold and passes them off to Coty. "Take these or they'll be confetti by the time she reaches you."

Beckett moves to my other side, then they each take a hand in one of theirs.

"Now you can't fidget," Beckett explains.

"Do not!" I shout, willing the sudden tears away. "Do not make me cry right now."

Marc shoves Coty's chest, telling him, "Get back over there so we can bring you your wife."

"It hurts," Coty says seriously.

Marc nods. "I know it does, man, but we'll return her to you safe and sound."

One-handed, Beckett pretends to dust the front of his *Keep Calm and Ride It* biker shirt, and mutters, "I'm not making that promise. There could be a rattlesnake out here or something."

"Oh my God!" I cry the same time Marc says, "Shut the fuck *up*."

Coty shakes his head, grinning, then turns to finally leave.

"I'm just kidding, Angie."

I side-eye Beckett. There absolutely are rattlesnakes in this canyon. I'm hoping none in this particular region at this particular time, but it's always a possibility. The thought of accidentally stepping on one under my dress has already gone through my mind. On repeat. At least I'm wearing my triple-black Adidas Cloudfoams.

He laughs, adding, "I'd totally pee on you if you got bit."

Marc's head shakes beside me. "That's a jellyfish sting, dumbass." In a pair of aviators, he's wearing a gray crewneck with the sleeves pushed up to his elbows and black jeans. Even though Coty and I dressed up, we didn't want anyone else to feel like they had to.

I squeeze their hands tight in mine, telling them, "Never

change." Their personalities are the same at thirty-one as they were at twenty-one, and I hope things will always be like this between us—the banter but also the acceptance.

"Neighbor girl's all grown up," Marc says, kissing my head.

"Yeah," Beckett agrees quietly before giving a matching kiss to the other side.

The tears actually fall this time, and I try to stop, just for a brief second, to let it all wash over me. I'm safe. I'm where I belong. I'm home.

CHAPTER 12

Coty

THE SUN IS JUST STARTING TO LOWER, CLOSER TO the horizon and bathing all the land in a gold-like haze. The long grass has already lost its color from the summer heat, so it looks like we're in a never-ending wheat field with random pops of wildflowers mixed in. With our cars parked haphazardly around us, and a lug nut acting as my temporary wedding band, we managed to stick to the theme Angela suggested after all.

She didn't tell me the songs she chose. She just took charge of the playlist and told me to listen carefully. I try to do exactly that as a cover of "Truly Madly Deeply" by a woman I've never heard before plays while Angela, Beck, and Marc make their way around Angela's Jeep, but it's hard to focus on anything other than my bride.

Holy shit.

Even though I've already memorized the striking deep-purple and black backless dress, I still can't take my eyes off her in it. On her worst days, Angela looks beautiful. Today, she looks out of this world. She is out of this world. She's my heaven.

With her standing about twenty yards away from me, and our close family surrounding us, I've never felt so full. No, not full. Fulfilled. Everything I've ever wanted is in this field today, and it's better than I could've imagined. I always knew I wanted a family of my own. I just never knew the path I'd be taking to get one. It's a path most people probably find unconventional, but since I've never given a shit about tradition or what other people think, it's been fucking perfect for me.

I told Angela all those years ago that I wanted messy, and fuck, did I get it. Our life is a messy, busy, chaotic, loud, dirty masterpiece, and Angela and I painted every single brushstroke together.

Hand in hand with my two best friends, she starts walking, coming right toward me at an agonizing pace. I swear Beck even stops several times just to test my patience. Fucker.

Off to the side, Blaze and Terra chase Jace around in a circle since there aren't any chairs out here, while Rebel smirks at Hunter glaring at her. Next to him is Beck's boy, Harley, who's bumping his shoulder into Makya's. Brittni is planted directly between Bentlee and Paige, with eyes that touch on everyone.

As soon as Angela and I made it into Beck's house, I pulled her and her sister aside to have our own little talk. I promised them both that I'll always be here, no matter what my official title is; that nobody will ever come between us again because we are a family, even if it's not a typical one; that they have nothing to fear anymore because I'll chase away every single one that comes along, and if I can't, I'll find a way around it like I do every other obstacle put in front of me.

It's gonna take time though, particularly for Brit. She's still guarded right now because she thinks this is temporary, just like foster care was. It's not. There's nothing temporary about the way our family loves. Just like it was with Angela, the road to helping Brittni trust real love won't be easy, but I've never backed down from putting in a little extra work, especially when it comes to my family.

Eventually my bride makes it to where I'm posted, her

hazel eyes never straying from mine. I hold the paper flowers out to Drew, but he doesn't take them. He just whispers, "What am I supposed to do with that?"

Not having any idea what the fuck I'm supposed to do with it either, I toss the whole bouquet out to my side, in the direction of our small audience. Both my hands now free, I practically rip Angela from my boys' hold, barely letting them each get a kiss on her cheek. I warned them I was taking her. She's. Mine.

"Ooh, Ty. Looks like you're getting married next."

What?

Angela and I turn toward the commotion to see all four of Paige's brothers joining the group, Ty holding the bouquet with a shocked expression. I guess he caught it.

Ty chucks it at Caleb, who immediately tosses it to Nick.

"Nicky's getting married," his sister singsongs, making the youngest Christensen brother lob it directly at her.

Thanks to those long legs, Beck makes it to his wife's rescue in record time, intercepting the flowers and saying, "Don't think so, man. This one's taken," then flings it at the oldest, Jesse.

The brothers perform another round of Hot Potato with their sister's handmade creation, paper petals flying in the wake of every pass before pitifully fluttering to the ground. The diversion allows the parents to corral all their kids.

Beck and Paige gather Harley and Terra, along with their cousin, Diesel.

With Blaze already in one arm, Marc uses the other to take Makya's hand and lead her over to stand next to her older sister. Brittni cracks a smile at something Bentlee's whispering near her ear, and Hunter joins his parents, putting himself in view of Blaze so he can interpret the ceremony for her.

Behind them, Rebel gives Karina an exasperated look like she can't believe she was pulled away from riding for this shit.

I don't know which Christensen ends up with the bouquet, but they position themselves among everybody else, blending in seamlessly.

I shake my head and grin. Fuck, I love our life.

Angela smiles back at me. "Ready to be my husband?"

"I was ready like nine and a half years ago." Longer, but she probably already knows that.

"You're crazy."

"You're beautiful."

Her lips stretch so wide, I feel mine mimic the move.

Drew reads from his phone, skipping over parts that we groan at, and getting to the only part we actually care about.

"Coty, do you take Angela—"

"I do."

"Okay… Angela, do you—"

"I do."

Angela's ex-stepbrother sighs. "Why did I even bother downloading this script at all? Screw it. Rings, please."

Angela chuckles at Drew's irritated yet polished tone while I pull out her ring and my…lug nut.

Drew eyes my hexagonal-shaped ring as he says, "Let these rings serve as symbols of not only your love and devotion to each other, but also your promise to have and to hold and to *never* let go." *I told him to add that part.*

"Never," I say, sliding hers on.

Without blinking, Angela repeats, "Never," and guides my lug nut down my ring finger.

My cock tries to stiffen in my suit pants, but I shut that shit down. We'll get there, just not right this minute.

"It is my honor to pronounce you husband and wife. You may kiss your—"

My lips meet Angela's in the middle and we kiss like it's our first time all over again except we're no longer strangers, or neighbors—we're motherfucking husband and wife.

Cheers from our family erupt and some of them even clap, but still, I kiss my wife, ignoring the rest of the world.

It's only when Jace yells, "Daddy, Mommy can't breathe!" that I break the kiss.

"Is that true?"

She shrugs with a sated smile. "I figured you'd be the death of me."

I give her another peck, laughing against her lips, then we turn to face our family, holding our conjoined hands high in the air.

We gaze at each other, and Angela says, "Sweetest demise I could ever hope for."

"I'm just getting started," I promise her with a wink.

This morning I woke up in a spare bed, missing half of my existence, but tonight I'll go to sleep in my own bed, with my own wife, with our kids just across the hall from us, and every-thing—*everything*—will be exactly the way it's supposed to be.

I chased after this moment like it was our final destina-tion, but now that we're here, it's not an end at all, it's just the beginning.

This is our beginning.

Want to see exactly how Angela got payback on the Creekwood men?
Read the bonus scene here:
https://bit.ly/3UhSvVv

Check out my website amarieauthor.com for playlists, inspiration boards, and up-to-date news.

BOOKS BY A. MARIE

Creekwood Series

Detour

Changing Lanes

Blind Spot

Roundabout

Standalones

Let The Light Shine Through

The Comedown

ACKNOWLEDGMENTS

Thanks to all the readers who have fallen as deeply for this world as I have. It's been my absolute pleasure bringing these characters to life. I hope their stories have given you the same escape they've given me.

Thank you to the entire team who helped with this one: Murphy, Sarah, Judy, Shanna, Amanda, and Stacey.

And special thanks to a few of my awesome newsletter subscribers—Elise, Shanna, and Whitney—for helping name the goats.